CINNAMON SPICED OMEGA

THE HOLLYDALE OMEGAS BOOK 2

SUSI HAWKE

Cupid always gives you a second chance...

Alpha's Dream: Book 1

Omega Found: Book 2

Omega's Destiny: Book 3

Alpha's Dom: Book 4

Alpha's Charm: Book 5

Omega's Mark: Book 6

Alpha's Seal: Book 7

The Hollydale Omegas

Pumpkin Spiced Omega: Book 1

Cinnamon Spiced Omega: Book 2

Peppermint Spiced Omega: Book 3

Champagne Spiced Omega: Book 4

Chocolate Spiced Omega: Book 5

Shamrock Spiced Omega: Book 6

Marshmallow Spiced Omega: Book 7

Three Hearts Collection
(with Harper B. Cole)

The Surrogate Omega: Book 1

The Divorced Omega: Book 2

This book is dedicated to all of the kind people who helped a poor family thirty years ago that had nowhere to go on Thanksgiving nor a warm home to enjoy the holiday. May we live to see a day where nobody is cold, homeless, and without basic human comforts.

S.H.

CHAPTER 1

CHRISTIAN

"It's the head gasket, sir. I'm going to need another day before your car will be ready." I was looking over my schedule, while I balanced the phone on my ear.

The man's irate voice let out a stream of profanities before finally sighing and asking: "I assume this means that the higher estimate you quoted is the one I'm looking at now."

Returning my focus to the matter at hand, I agreed and quoted the new estimate. I finished our conversation and hung up the phone. It was always a bitch to give people bad news about their cars, but at least I could usually fix the problem. Eventually.

I took a drink of coffee, irritated to notice that it had gone cold. After I quickly updated the file for the repair that had just been authorized, I stood and went back out to the garage. An old Kansas tune was blasting in the cavernous space, joining the cacophony of the other sounds that filled my workday.

The clamor of a metal tool hitting the cement floor when Scott dropped a wrench over by Mr. Tso's Prius, the impact gun Neal was currently using to remove the lug nuts from Mrs. Peterman's Buick, the revving engine coming from '78 Camaro where Tim was checking the carburetor: these were the sounds of my world.

Tim poked his head around the hood, wiping his hands on the shop rag that hung from the pocket of his navy coveralls. "Hey, boss man. Are we a go on the Dodge? I already talked to Dennis over at the machine shop, they can fit us in first thing tomorrow for the head resurfacing. I told him I'd drop it off by the end of the day if you gave the thumbs up."

"Sounds good, Tim. Both thumbs way up, we're definitely a go. He wasn't thrilled, but can't say I blame him. He's already sunk a lot into that old beater."

"True. But once he gets past all this, it's gonna be a good, solid ride for his kid. Hell, it's gonna be too much car for the kid if you ask me." Tim smirked at the old muscle car parked over in bay five. "With a good restoration job and a complete overhaul on the engine, that car would be my baby. I'd never need to get laid again. That car would be enough to do it for me."

Chuckling, I shook my head. "Yeah, well, instead it will be doing it for a teen-aged alpha. I don't know how much his dad plans to fix it up, but he did mention it's getting painted next week."

Tim shook his head and turned back to the Camaro. "Well, shit. That kid won't be sitting home on Friday nights. He's pretty much guaranteed to get all the action he wants if they do even a half decent job painting it. Those little omegas will go nuts over him."

"I imagine they already are, since he's on the football team. Oh, well. Forget the kid. Tell me some good news about this Camaro. I need to call the owner for an update. He's already left two messages this morning."

"Sure thing, Chris. It's not as bad as we'd expected. Come on over, let me walk you through it."

After he filled me in, I went back to the office to call the customer. The rest of the morning flew by, one car or customer at a time. At lunch time, I dragged myself out of the office and decided to go check in on my kid brother over at Sweet Ballz where he'd worked since high school.

I'd opened Greasy Fingers Garage here in Hollydale about five years ago. I had moved home to take care of my kid brother after our omega dad died. Neither of us knew our alpha fathers. It had always just been the three of us. The three amigos. The three musketeers. It had been a ballsy move to open my own business with my share of the meager life insurance our dad had left for us, especially for a kid just barely old enough to drink.

I had needed the income to take care of my brother, and mechanics was what I knew. When I saw that the town had no decent garage, it had seemed like a no-brainer. Luckily, it had paid off. Now I had a good staff and a steady stream of customers. My brother had been able to finish high school and never needed to worry about having a roof over his head.

Kent was six years younger than me. He was twenty now, but still so young in so many ways. His job at the candy shop was a perfect fit for him. My dad would've loved to know that his younger alpha son made a living making candy. It was so different from the career paths that most alphas took. Kent was a gentler alpha though. He was a sweet kid, with none of the normal alpha characteristics, at least not so far. Maybe he just hadn't come in to his own yet.

I headed out the backdoor of the garage, ducking through the alley that separated my garage from the backside of the row of shops where Sweet Ballz was located. As I passed the row of dumpsters that served the different businesses, an old man stepped out from between two of them.

Jumping back, I willed myself to calm down and breathe. The old dude looked harmless enough but his sudden appearance had scared the shit out of me. He was shorter than me, his head about level with my shoulder. The sunlight sparkled against his shiny bald head, highlighting the wispy white hairs that grew in sparse little patches around the sides and back of his head.

He was about two days past shaving, with a grizzled white stubble covering his wrinkled jaw. I looked into his surprisingly sharp blue eyes that twinkled merrily. The old guy was grinning like a loon, his yellowed teeth flashing.

"Whoa, there! You kids are always in hurry. Almost stopped my heart, you coming up like that."

I grinned back at him. "I think you have that backwards, sir. I'm pretty sure that I'm the one who almost had the heart attack with the way that you jumped out at me."

He chuckled with the breathy rasp of a lifetime smoker. "Sorry, kid. And the name's Otis, no need to bother with that sir shit. What are you doing back here anyway, kid?" Otis dug around in the pocket of his crackled leather jacket, looking for something. No old man cardigans for this guy, he even wore his khakis at his natural waist level, instead of up to his armpits like most old timers.

"Okay, Otis. I'm Chris. I own the shop back there," I pointed a thumb over my shoulder in the direction of my shop. I wasn't entirely sure why I'd extended the conversation, but I continued. "I haven't seen you around here before, Otis. Are you new in town?"

Otis finally found what he was looking for as he triumphantly pulled a partially smoked cigar out of his pocket. He lit it and gave a few satisfied puffs before answering me. I took a polite step to the side, hoping to get out of the path of his smoke.

"Not new, no. Just don't get around as much as I used to, I suppose." He spoke around the fat cigar that was now nestled in the corner of his mouth. He eyes glinted with humor, as though laughing at a private joke.

"Oh, I see. Well, it was nice to meet you, Otis. I'm actually headed over to have lunch with my kid brother. Can I bring you anything? Or would you like to join us?" Again, I had no idea why I'd offered that, but the satisfied gleam in his eye told me that it had been the right thing to say.

"Ha! I knew you were a good kid. I always was a good judge of character. Nah, kid. I'm good. I'll be around for awhile, so we'll see each other again. Count on it."

It felt like I was being dismissed, so I took the hint. "Alright, Otis. Well, it was nice to meet you. I'm right over there in the Greasy Fingers Garage if you ever need to find me. I'd better get going before I run out of time for lunch."

With a grin and a wave, I hurried on down the alley and ducked into the backdoor of the kitchen where

Kent would be busy rolling balls or melting chocolate. Today he was rolling doughy balls, with the help of the store manager, Tom.

Tom looked up as I came in the door. As I pulled it shut behind me, he gave me the once over and pointed to the sink. "As much as Tom loves a grease covered alpha, Christian must wash up first."

I grinned. "Well, I washed my hands before I came over, but no problem. This is a kitchen, I get it. Do you want me to take off the coveralls or put on an apron?"

Tom fanned his face. "What does Christian have on under those coveralls? Do not disappoint Tom, alpha."

I slowly lowered my zipper with a teasing grin, enjoying the way the bossy little omega eyed me as I removed them to reveal a tight-fitting tank top and running shorts. I laid them on the counter by the back-door with a shrug. "What? It gets hot under those but I don't wear them when Kent and I go to lunch. So, yeah. Light clothes underneath."

Kent's head came up then. He looked over at the clock and back down at the table in front of him, before turning to look at me with wide eyes. "I'm sorry, Chun! I lost track of time. There's no way I can leave right now. This order needs to get done by five."

I smiled at the childhood nickname Kent insisted on calling me. When he was little, he couldn't say Christian. Instead, it had come out as 'Chun' and had stuck within our family ever since. "It's okay, Kent. I'll be happy to run and grab us all sandwiches from next door if you want?"

Tom gave me another slow elevator eye treatment. "Tom will call in an order. Christian can help Kent play with his balls."

He and I both snickered. Seriously, when Kent's boss had named this place he obviously hadn't been thinking about all the ball jokes that would just roll off the tongue. Even the name. Sweet Ballz? It was epic. I grinned at Tom and went over to take his place as he got up to go order our usual from the Sub Shoppe next door. Seriously. It was named Sub Shoppe. This town and its names. That's why I'd gone for the tongue in cheek name Greasy Fingers when I'd named my garage. Not only did I get to laugh at the pun, I fit right in with the rest of the businesses.

Kent was barely noticing me as he deftly rolled the little balls of dough and lined them up on the paper covered trays that were arranged in the center of the large metal island where we were working. I began rolling the balls, making sure they were the same size as the others or Kent would freak out on me. I'd made that mistake before.

"Hey, Kent. What are these? They smell interesting. Almost like apple pie."

Kent's head came up, his eyes lit with excitement. "I

know! This is for a special fall party at the apple orchard. They're celebrating the new cider recipe and asked me to use the cider in a hands-free dessert. This is a basic cookie dough, done with the apple cider and little bits of apple. Once we're done rolling them, I'll bake them. After they're cool, I'm dipping them in cinnamon infused white chocolate."

I shook my head, amazed at his creativity. "And you came up with this recipe yourself?"

Kent shrugged. "Milo and I were spit-balling ideas after the order came in. I suggested this idea. We tried a few different recipes until we ended up with this one. They're actually really good. It's like a mix of a snicker-doodle and apple pie, if I had to describe it. They will be more like a cookie ball then a candy ball, but that's fine. We're calling them Cider Ballz."

My stomach growled then, making us both laugh. "Can I just ask you to save me a few? I really need to try these. You know how much I love cinnamon. And apples. Damn, Kent. These are my dessert version of a wet dream."

As if my words had conjured him, Tom popped through the swinging door from the main shop right then. He held a bag of sandwiches in the crook of his arm, and a big grin on his face. "Oooh. Tom arrived just in time. Christian needs to tell Tom more about these wet dreams."

I tossed him a wink and went back to rolling balls. I figured we'd be done in about five minutes and then I could dig into the food Tom held. "Is there more dough to roll, Kent? Or will we be done after this last bit?"

Kent shook his head. "No, this is the last of it. As soon as we get them all done, I'll slip the first batch into the oven and we can eat."

Tom slid onto the stool beside me and waited for us to finish while he scrolled on his phone. I spent another half hour with them. As soon as I finished eating, I reluctantly slid my coveralls back on so I could head back to work. As pleasant as these little breaks with my brother were, I had a business to run. I said good-bye to Tom and reminded Kent to bring some of those amazing Cider Ballz home with him tonight.

While I was walking back down the alley, I thought back to my earlier meeting with the interesting old guy. It didn't surprise me that Otis was long gone. I just wondered if I'd ever see him again, and what his story was anyway. When I passed the spot where I'd met him, a large feather caught my eye. I bent down and picked it up.

It was a pristine white quill feather with golden edges. The feather was long and wide. It looked just like the ones used for, well, feather pens. I held it up, admiring its beauty. There was no way this came from a bird. It had to have blown here from someone who used it for crafts or designs of some sort. It was too beautiful to be found in nature.

I was still holding it when I walked into my office. I laid it on the shelf where I kept photos of my family from when we were younger. My dad would've loved this feather. Fanciful bits of fluff had been his thing. Smiling, I gave it one last glance and went back to work. I had customers to deal with, parts to order, and a garage full of cars waiting to be fixed.

CHAPTER 2

LIAM

I looked around the cutesy little town that my last ride had dropped me off in after I'd become too nauseous to keep moving. It was because I was hungry. When I got hungry to a certain point, I always got nauseous. Even at three and a half months pregnant, I was already round enough that people felt sorry for me and didn't mind picking up a hitchhiker. Even one with bruises on every visible bit of skin and a black, swollen eye. The fact that I was only 5'1 and on the skinny side didn't hurt either. I was pretty much the least threatening hitchhiker out there.

Gene would be looking for me, but after hopping three states in two days between who knew how many different cars, I was probably safe enough. For now. My biggest concern at the moment was finding food. With only $11 left in my wallet, I needed to figure something out soon. The alpha who had dropped me off three, maybe four, car rides back had insisted on making me take his warm winter coat. That was a godsend, for sure.

I shoved my hands into its deep pockets and hunched into it for warmth as I walked. I felt a crinkle of paper in my left pocket. Pulling my hand out, I found a crisp $100 bill. Glancing around quickly, I shoved it back into my pocket and tried to make sense of it. It must have been that last ride. The lady had been concerned about me, she'd probably stuffed it in there as I was getting out of her car.

Shaking my head, my heart a lot lighter now, I looked around for a place to find some food. When I noticed a sign that read Sub Shoppe with a picture of a huge sandwich, I decided to treat myself and the baby in my belly. Tomorrow I would look around and see if there were any shelters or places to find help in this town. But for now, I just wanted to get some food in me and find a place to curl up out of sight.

After purchasing a combo deal of a footlong veggie sandwich and a bottle of apple juice, I ducked around the back of the row of shops. Usually, the nicer areas like this had a place with all their dumpsters lined up together. The wall of dumpsters would form a nice, if smelly, wall to hide behind while I slept.

Sure enough, I found a square alley behind the row of shops. There was another row of shops backing onto the alley as well. That row was lined up in a perpendicular row that ran along the left side of the square, with a neat row of dumpsters on the right side. They backed up to an eight-foot-high cement sound wall, with bushy shrubs growing in front of it. This would be a perfect place for me hide out and finally catch my breath after my long flight of terror.

Maybe not the most comfortable, but who needed comfort? Nope. All I needed was to finally be able to sleep without fear. This area felt strangely peaceful to me. I had almost decided to hitch a ride later out of here when my stomach settled, but I felt almost compelled to stay now.

I wasn't looking where I was going as I crossed the alley, and somehow managed to bump right into the quite muscular chest of a large man that was heading the way I'd just come from. I bounced off him and landed right on my ass. The bag holding my sandwich landed on the asphalt beside me.

"Whoopsies, sorry about that! Are you okay?" I looked up into a pair of soulful brown eyes. My neck craned back as I looked up at the alpha towering over me. Gulping, I shied away from him. I was ashamed at how I cowered, but I knew from experience the pain that large alpha hands like his could cause. It didn't matter that he smelled like tart apples. No, smell didn't say anything about a man.

"I-I'm sorry, alpha. I wasn't paying attention." I made myself look him in the eye, watching him carefully as I tried to judge his intentions. We were alone in an empty alley, after all. His eyes widened as he took in my bruised face and then moved down to take in my round belly that protruded between the open flaps of my coat.

"Call me Christian, or Chris. And don't worry about it, please. I think we were both lost in thought. Are you sure you're okay? You took a hard fall there, and with a baby on board too."

He smiled kindly as he reached a hand out to help me up. Unable to politely refuse, I took his hand and allowed him to pull me to my feet. Once I was steady, he leaned down and snagged the bag I'd dropped.

Handing it to me, he asked: "Can I at least buy you another sandwich? The Sub Shoppe food is too good to let it get ruined from being on the ground."

Knowing full well that I would soon be on the ground myself, I hardly cared about the food bag having dropped there. I snorted out a half-giggle at the thought.

Looking back up at him, I said politely: "No, really, it's fine. The sandwich is wrapped well and inside a bag, there's no way that it was hurt. The only thing hurt here is my pride. Thank you though."

He nodded pensively, obviously wanting to do more for me, but not wanting to press. "And you promise that you're not just saying that to be polite? You're okay?"

"I'm okay, I promise." I pulled the bottle of juice from my pocket and held it up. "See, even my drink didn't break."

Smiling now, Christian said: "Okay, I guess I'll let you get on with your evening then. But first, tell me your name. If you don't mind? I just don't want to think of you as the pregnant omega that I knocked over because I was lost in thought."

I blushed but answered readily. "My name is Liam. It's nice to meet you."

Christian smiled, his white teeth shining against his tanned face and darkly stubbled chin. "Liam. What a lovely name. Well, forgive me again for knocking you down. If you ever need anything, I own the garage over there at the end of the driveway."

He turned and pointed to the end of the row of shops and businesses. I saw a few garage doors down on the end. I just nodded.

"Thank you, Christian. Well, I better get going now," I said and wiggled my bag with a smile.

With a nod, he smiled and went on his way. I watched him go with a wistful pang in my heart. Why couldn't I have met an alpha like him instead of Gene? I couldn't imagine the man I'd just met ever laying his hands on an omega in anger. And wow, he'd smelled so good!

With a sad sigh, I looked around carefully before

ducking back behind the dumpsters. I was halfway back when I noticed a cute old man with a bald spot on the top of his head sitting on the curb ahead of me. He was leaning against the sound wall, his legs stretched out in front of him, ankles crossed. He looked up at me and smiled.

"Hello, Liam. Come join me, kiddo." He chewed on an unlit cigar as he patted the curb next to him. I hesitated, although there was a peaceful aura around him that urged me forward.

"How do you know my name?" I asked curiously, not at all afraid of this adorable man. "I've never been here before. I don't even know the name of this town, but you know mine?"

"Relax, kiddo. I heard you introducing yourself to that nice young alpha out there. You'd be surprised at the things you can pick up if you're paying attention." He smiled kindly and patted the curb again insistently.

With a mental shrug, I went over and eased my sore body down next to him. My stomach gurgled, reminding me of my hunger.

"Go ahead and eat your dinner, Liam. I'm just gonna keep you company for a bit, before I move on for the night."

I opened the bag and pulled out my sandwich, not needing to be told twice. Remembering my manners, I held up the wrapped food. "Can I offer you half? I'm not going to eat it all in one sitting anyway. It's veggie though, I ordered this one so that I wouldn't have to worry about saving it." I'd really wanted the ham and swiss but knew it would be wasted without refrigeration for the other half.

"You know what, Liam? I think I'll take you up on that. It's been too long since I've eaten...err, a sandwich." I glanced over his strange hesitation but shrugged it off and passed him half of the food.

I didn't look before I bit into it, so I was amazed to find myself with a mouth full of ham and swiss with a hint of mayo. They must have goofed up my sandwich, although I couldn't figure out how when I'd watched the guy make it and carry it to the girl at the register. And there weren't any other customers there, so maybe it was intended for one of them?

The old man must have sensed my confusion, because he winked at me and said: "Don't you just love surprises? I love happy accidents and surprise endings."

I smiled happily and nodded as I dug into another bite. Making myself slow down so I wouldn't get sick, I counted to thirty with each bite. The sandwich was still gone before I knew it anyway, and I was crumpling up the wrapper and putting it back in the bag. I set the bag on the ground between us and reached into my pocket for my juice. I hesitated, not sure how to split this one.

The old man smiled gently and said: "Oh, good. I'm

glad you chose an organic juice. Your daughter needs the vitamins, not a load of chemical bullshit." He winked and pulled a bottle of water out of his own jacket pocket, tipping it in my direction like a toast before drinking.

After I took a few sips of juice, I said: "So, you think I'm having a girl, huh?"

"Know. Not think. There's a difference, kiddo. Never make a claim that you can't back up. And kiddo? You have girl just written all over that belly of yours." He winked at me and flashed yellowed teeth as he grinned around his stogie.

I leaned back against the wall, suddenly exhausted as the strain from the past few days lifted. My belly was full. Even though I was outside on chilly November night, I felt at peace. What felt like only a few minutes later, I opened my eyes as a soft bundle landed on my lap.

Blinking drowsily, I opened my eyes to see a fluffy pillow on my lap. On the ground in front of me was a sleeping bag. The old guy was standing there smiling down at me.

"Sorry to wake you, sleeping beauty. It's gonna get cold later, spread that out and get warm. No use freezing out here."

"No, no. I couldn't possibly take your things. Uh-uh. Thank you, but I'm younger and I have a good coat." I tried to hand the pillow to him, but he just shook his head.

"Trust me, kiddo. I ain't got no use for them things. Those are for you. Get some sleep now. You'll be safe back here for as long as you're meant to be." He grinned around that stogie again.

"Um. Okay, if you're sure. Thank you, um, wait. I don't even know your name!" I was horrified that I'd been so rude as to not have gotten such an important piece of basic information from the sweet old timer.

He was already turning to walk away but looked back over his shoulder and said. "The name's Otis. Don't worry, kiddo. Like I said, you're safe here. Hollydale's a good place, you'll see. But if you need me, don't worry. I'll be around."

I looked down at the pillow, overcome by his kindness. I moved the pillow to the curb beside me and saw a fresh bottle of water standing there too. I looked up to thank him, but he was already gone. I jumped up and stepped out between the dumpsters to catch him, but there was no sign of him. I shook my head. What a weird night. Well, at least I knew the name of this town now. Hollydale. Hmm. It did sound nice.

CHAPTER 3

CHRISTIAN

Kent and I were sitting in front of the TV watching the new episode of The Omega Bachelor, a stupid dating show that my brother never missed. It involved one omega and a group of alphas competing for the right to take him as a mate and marry him. It wasn't my thing, but that didn't matter. I was happy to see my brother happy.

I knew if I went by the shop that Kent and Tom would be talking about it at work tomorrow. They were both rabid fans of the show. Tom was even talking about sending in an audition video to be the next Omega Bachelor.

While my brother oohed and aahed at his show, my mind was running over my encounter earlier with that poor little omega. Liam. When he'd first bumped into me, I'd been distracted by the heavenly smell of cinnamon. I was wondering if Kent was making something good and maybe it was wafting from the vent when we'd ran into each other.

When he'd cowered from me in fear, my heart had broken a little. He'd curled up in on himself there on the ground, his nearly shoulder length hair a tangled curtain around his face. The shitty part was when I'd realized that my size, and the fact that I'm an alpha, is what was scaring him.

But when he'd looked up at me, so brave despite his fright? Oh, man. I was impressed. I'd been captivated by the intelligent green eyes that sparkled, despite the fear in that bruised face. I had wanted to ask if he needed protection, but the look in his eyes told me not to go there. Not yet anyway.

The only thing that had kept me from taking more action, was the fact that the bruises were all at the purpling stage. That seemed to suggest that they were a couple days old now. Presumably, the punk that did them wasn't around since the little guy had been blithely walking through the alley.

Who the fuck would hurt a tiny omega like Liam anyway? If I ever met the guy, I would have to show him how it felt to have someone fuck you up like that. I hadn't seen a ring on the omega's finger, not that it meant anything. Still. I had a sinking feeling that Liam was alone and pregnant.

As much as I hoped that wasn't true, I just had a bad

feeling that the guy needed someone in his corner. I would be keeping my eye out for the guy. If he did need help, hopefully he would accept mine. I mean, if it wasn't too weird for him that an alpha he'd never met before today wanted to take care of him. I couldn't explain it really, I was just drawn to the guy. I'd never really been interested in finding an omega, but if I had? Liam would be just my type.

The next couple days dragged by, and I didn't see Liam anywhere. I kept catching that spicy scent of cinnamon, but not the omega himself. He had to be nearby, I just couldn't figure out where. I'd even asked Kent and Tom to keep an eye out for him. There had naturally been a flurry of questions from Tom on the matter.

Once I'd described Liam, he'd been ready to send out a search party himself. It had been sweet to see the flirty little guy stalk off muttering about poor omegas and abusive alphaholes. I'd always thought there was more to Tom than met the eye, this show of empathy just helped prove it to me.

On the third day, I walked into my office after dealing with a transmission problem on the mayor's car. Otis was sitting in my chair, his feet propped up on my desk. Unable to summon anything but a grin, I sat down in my guest chair.

"How are you doing, Otis. Fancy meeting you here."

Otis grinned around his cigar, his grizzled stubble completing the picture. "Hey, sonny boy. How's tricks? I decided it was about time to run you down, see what's going on with you."

I raised an eyebrow with a smirk. "Well. I was about to get to work, but apparently, I'm entertaining a guest. How are you, Otis? Did you need something?"

Otis dropped his feet to the floor and sat up. He smacked the desktop with the flat of his hand. "Yes! Thanks for asking, sonny boy. I do need something. I need for you to get yourself out of your rut. Work and home. Home and work. Your only detour is the lunch breaks you take with the kid brother."

I leaned back in my chair, surprised that this odd little man knew such intimate details about my hum-drum routine. He was right though, I was definitely in a rut.

"I'm not even gonna ask how you know all that, Otis. Or how you got into my office without me or any of my guys seeing you. I have a feeling I wouldn't like the answer to any questions you could give me anyway. So, I won't bother. Is there anything in particular that you'd care to suggest that I do with this rut that you've found me in?"

"I thought you'd never ask, sonny boy. Now, have you ever thought of giving back? Getting out and doing something for those that can't do for themselves?"

I nodded. "Actually. Yeah, I have. My dad," I glanced over at our family picture up on the shelf. "My dad was a good guy that worked his ass off to keep a roof over our heads and food in our mouths. Many times, we got food from the local food pantry, and clothes from the church poor bin."

Smiling fondly, I added: "One of the best Thanksgiving meals we ever had was one we went to at the church down the street. We couldn't afford the turkey and all the trimmings that year. And we'd missed the day they gave out Thanksgiving food boxes because my dad was working a double at the diner. But the church dinner? They were so kind. The people treated us all like guests, not like needy charity cases. I never felt so much kindness as a kid."

I shook my head with a startled grin and said: "I don't know why I just told you all that, Otis. You have a way of making people talk, do you know that? Shit. Another thirty seconds and you'd have had me singing Kumbaya."

Otis chuckled with a rasping wheeze. "That's okay, sonny boy. I don't need no serenades." He leaned in closer, his arms resting on my desk in front of him. "You know, they still do those dinners? Yep. They surely do. Those people leave their own homes on the holiday and go down to serve up dinner for the poor and home-less. Many of the people who come to that dinner wouldn't eat that day if it wasn't for those volunteers."

I chewed my lip thoughtfully as I considered his words. "But, Otis. I don't belong to that church. Hell, I don't even go to church. I'm pretty sure they wouldn't want me there. I'm not exactly church material, you know?"

Otis twisted his lip around the cigar. "Sonny boy, if they wouldn't want you there, then they got no business bein' there themselves. Church is supposed to be come as you are and do unto others. This shit of people tryin' ta be holier than thou and judge everyone else is just that: shit. Naw. You belong there, boy. Trust me. The people down there are just grateful for any spare pair of hands willing to pitch in. They got a lot of people to serve, probably a couple hundred at least."

I raised my eyebrows and let out a low whistle. "There are that many needy people in Hollydale? I thought growing up that my family was the only poor one in this picturesque little burg of ours. Do you think they could use more help? My brother would definitely want to come along, I'm sure of it."

Otis smiled, his yellowed teeth on full view. "That's the spirit, sonny boy. Here's a card, ask for Micah. Tell him I sent you." He stood and dropped a card on my desk.

I reached over for it, studying it for a minute. "Micah, huh? I'll give him a call in a few..." I looked up, but Otis was gone. How the hell had he gotten out of here so fast? And was I really so out of it that I didn't even see or hear him pass me?

Shaking my head, I got up and went around to take my seat. I saw the gold tipped white feather on the floor in front of my chair. Huh. Otis must have been looking at it before I came in.

I still hadn't figured out where it came from. I'd stopped by the craft store a couple of days ago to ask what kind of feather it was, but they had no idea. The ones they carried were all cheaply made compared to this one. I picked it up, admiring it again. Reaching up to put it back on the shelf, my hand stilled mid-air.

The feather from a few days ago still sat there where I'd left it. The one in my hand was a completely different feather. What the fuck? My hand shook as I placed this one with the other. Otis was obviously at the center of the feather question.

I just couldn't wrap my brain around that crusty old guy carrying delicate feathers around with him. And where did he even keep them? They were at least 10" long, and not very bendy. I'm sure there was a logical explanation, even if the goosebumps on the back of my neck were screaming otherwise.

Before I left for lunch, I took a few minutes to call Micah. As it happened, he was short several volunteers. Thanksgiving was less than a week away, and he had just had a group of five people pull out. He'd been scrambling to fill their spots. I told him I'd get back to him in an hour, but that I could probably fill at least two of those spots. After we hung up, I headed off to

Sweet Ballz to talk to my brother. It was time to give back to the community.

———

"Well, yeah. You shouldn't even have to ask. Of course, I'm on board, Chun." Kent looked up at me with a sad smile, obviously thinking of our dad.

"Tom wants to come too. Milo and Rafe told Tom to invite Kent and Christian for dinner at the haunted house, but Tom likes this idea better!" The little omega was bristling with excitement. Again, it occurred to me that there was more to this dude than he let on. "Hold on, Tom will phone Milo. What time is the church dinner?"

After I'd told him 4:00 pm, he nodded and started tapping the screen of his phone. Then he abruptly strode off, holding the phone to his ear. Kent watched him go with a smile. "That guy. He kills me. He's got a good heart though. Like Dad did."

I nodded with understanding. "I've noticed that. I was just thinking that there's more to him than he wants people to notice."

Kent grinned. "Exactly. I think we only notice because we're both around him a lot. Oh! Hey, that reminds me. Tom saw your omega this morning! He was in here getting a cup of coffee and a couple of PBF Bombz."

I sat up so fast that my knees knocked against the metal table. "Liam was here? Really? How did he look? Did he say where he was going? And he's not my omega, he's just a guy that I noticed. That's all. I just wanted to make sure he's okay."

Kent's mouth dropped open as he listened to me babble. "Chun. Holy Shit! I was joking when I called him your omega, but now I'm wondering. He's a cutie, by the way. That thick long hair? Nice. But he looked banged up, for sure."

"He had more bruises? Fuck. I thought he was safe. I should have..."

"Chun." Kent interrupted. "The bruises are at least a week old from the look of them. Definitely fading. I meant, he looked like he *HAD* been banged up. And I have an idea of where he was going, if you want to calm your shit and let me talk."

I was fascinated by this side of my brother. Usually Kent was a man of few words, even as a kid he hadn't liked to talk that much. Liam must have really made an impression on him.

"Anyway. I saw him through the door after Tom came back to tell me that he was out there at a table. I didn't actually get close to him. But Tom sat and talked to him for awhile. He sent him over to apply for a job at that thrift store that Dad used to take us to for clothes over on Second Street. You remember the place? Second Chances?"

I nodded. It was a nice little place with a clean stock of gently used goods. It would be a perfect job for a pregnant omega. "And that's all you know?"

"That's all Kent knows," Tom's voice said as he came in and sat down on the stool next to me. "Tom called over there and made sure that Liam will get the job."

I looked at Tom quizzically. Tom just shrugged with a faint blush on his cheeks. "Omegas look after their own. Tom's friend Cecil owns and runs the place. Cecil needs help, Liam needs a job. Problem solved. Now. Let Tom talk Turkey Day!"

Kent and I both were chuckling. Then Tom surprised me yet again. "Kent, Christian and Tom will have an early dinner at the haunted house. Then Milo and Rafe will round out the five-some for helping at the church dinner."

Tom smirked at my open-mouthed stare. "Christian needed five people, right? Tom got two more people. Now there are five. Go call the church, alpha." He slid off the stool and turned to go back out front. On his way out, he turned back and said with a sly smile: "By the way? Liam starts work at ten tomorrow morning. Cecil texted while Tom was talking to Milo."

My cheeks warmed when Kent started shaking his head and laughing at the happy look on my face. I didn't care though. Now I knew where to find the little omega that had been on my mind for days. And see if he really was the source of that fantastic cinnamon smell.

Kent commented dryly as I finished my lunch: "Well, I guess I'm on my own for lunch tomorrow. I imagine that you have a sudden need for second chance clothing? Maybe a used book or two? Actually, let's plan on it. I'll go with you. I wouldn't want you to look like a stalker. I'll be your wing man, if that's what that means."

I started to tell him no, but then I realized that maybe it wasn't such a bad idea to have my kid brother along. It would look a lot more innocent. More meet cute, less creepy stalker. "Okay. But if you aren't ready to go when I get here, I'm leaving without your ass."

CHAPTER 4

LIAM

Cecil was patiently showing me how to run the register. He was the sweetest omega. I'm pretty sure that he hired me simply because that amazing Tom had asked him to, but I didn't care. I was relieved to have a job. Maybe I'd be able to afford a room to rent before the snows came. I had already purchased a backpack and a couple outfits to put in it.

The employee discount that Cecil offered made it possible for me to finally have a change of clothes. When he'd offered yesterday, I'd jumped at the chance. After a week spent in the tight-fitting t-shirt and jeans that I'd been wearing the night I escaped Gene, I was happy to have fresh clothes on my body.

I'd stopped at the gas station on the way here this morning to take an ice-cold sink bath with paper towels and industrial pink hand soap. I hated the funky smell of it, but it felt good to be cleaner inside of my new outfit.

We were going over how to track and arrange deliveries for the larger items like furniture, when the bell over the door tinkled. I looked up as the scent of tart apples filled the air. That apple smell was definitely Christian. He looked and smelled every bit as delicious up close as I remembered.

I'd seen him so many times over the past week, walking through the alley every day at lunchtime to go do whatever it was he did before he made a return trip about an hour later. Every day, like clockwork. At the end of the day, he'd walk through again on his way home. I assumed he walked through in the mornings too, but I was usually asleep in my little hiding spot then.

I felt so safe there, that I didn't bother waking up super early to vacate. Except on Tuesdays. On Tuesday I'd heard the garbage truck entering the alley to empty the dumpsters. I'd ducked behind a bush with my stuff until it was gone. Now I knew that Tuesdays were early days for me. Other than weather worries, I had accidentally found a temporary safe space.

I hadn't come out when I'd seen Christian going by, even after I knew his routine. I'd been content to watch him pass, watching him and getting an idea of who he was when he thought nobody was watching. I knew he could smell me, I'd seen him look around and sniff the air more than once. I just hadn't been ready to talk to him yet.

But now, he was here. At my new job. With another kind looking alpha in tow. The other alpha was a bit younger but looked somewhat like him. They were obviously brothers, which made me feel even better. It was nice to see that the strong alpha was close to his family.

Both alphas glanced at me out of the corners of their eyes, but they hadn't said anything to me yet. Christian just gave me a quick nod with a friendly smile as they made their way over to the used book rack. Books? He liked to read? Yet another thing that piqued my interest in this alpha. I wasn't sure at all what to make of the guy, but I was definitely intrigued.

Cecil was looking over at me with a soft smile. He leaned over and whispered: "Which one are you so obviously not watching?"

With a blush, I opened my mouth to deny it. Instead, I found myself whispering: "The taller one is a really nice alpha that I met last week."

"Good." Cecil said with a wink. "That younger one has a tushie that I'd could bite like a plum."

I bit back a giggle but looking at the two butts that were currently facing us as they bent over the lower shelves on the bookcase, I had to agree. They both definitely had grade A tushies. Cecil elbowed me in the side with a wink, and we both had to turn around to stifle our giggles.

Cecil and I got back to work after that. It was a straight forward system. I knew there would be no problem arranging a delivery if my boss wasn't around. He then had me do a few sample invoices for the furniture sales until I felt confident that I could do those as well. The two brothers walked over to the counter right as I finished the last sample, both of them with at least a few books in hand.

I smiled shyly at Christian as he greeted me. "Hello, Liam. It's good to see you again. I'm glad to see your butt isn't broken after that fall the other day."

Cecil and the other alpha were looking at us with wide eyes as I giggled and replied: "I mean, there is a crack in it though. But I'm pretty sure it's meant to be there."

Christian's jaw dropped at my words right before he threw his head back and roared with laughter. Cecil was giggling along with him while the other alpha looked at Christian like he'd grown a second head.

At my curious look, the younger guy set down his books and held out a hand. "Hi, I'm Kent. And I am really happy to meet someone that can make my big brother laugh like that."

I shook his hand, making sure to keep my grip firm and

steady. "I'm Liam. It's nice to meet you. Do you work with your brother?"

Kent shook his head. "No, I work with Tom at Sweet Ballz. I'm the candy maker. Or baker. Whatever. You know, the guy in back making all the good stuff."

Cecil fluttered his lashes and leaned in to rest his elbows on the counter beside me. "Tell us more about the good stuff you make in back. I'm Cecil, by the way," he said flirtatiously. Kent's face flushed red with the most adorable blush from Cecil's attentions.

My boss took a hint and eased up on the poor shy alpha. "Seriously, though. I love the stuff you guys make there. I went to a party over at my cousin's orchard over the weekend. He had these things he called Cider Ballz? Holy cow, I was amazed!"

Kent blushed harder but Christian stepped in and bragged: "Kent came up with that recipe. I loved them too. I told him that I need those on the regular, right? At least during cider season. They tasted like a ball of fall, forgive the rhyme."

Cecil nodded excitedly. "Exactly! It was like apple pie and snickerdoodles in one little ball of deliciousness. Are you going to stock those in the store, Kent?" He turned to Kent with interest.

Nodding, Kent said: "Yes, but only for this week. My boss Milo thinks that we should carry them until

Thanksgiving. After that, we'll be switching over to Peppermint Ballz. Milo wants to do Eggnog Ballz too, so I'm playing with that recipe right now in my free time."

It was sweet how Kent came to life when talking about his baking. My stomach rumbled a little from hearing him talk. I'd treated myself to going into that shop, and it was the best thing I'd ever done. Tom, the funny omega that ran the place, had been the one to help me get this job.

Christian looked at me when my stomach rumbled. "Do you have a lunch break soon? I'd love to treat you, if you'd want to join me."

I tried to be demur, but Cecil jumped in. "No. That's a good idea, Liam. You've been working long enough to take a break. Go eat lunch and come back in an hour. This place doesn't get that busy until a little after lunch anyway."

Christian smiled at my boss. "Thanks. By the way, I love your store. You're too young to know this, but this is where my brother and I got all of our school clothes growing up. Except there was an older guy here then. Kind of grumpy, but a nice guy."

Cecil smiled sadly. "Yeah, that was my grandpa. This was his place. He raised me, I spent most of my childhood playing in this store. I took it over after he died."

"Oh, wow. I had no idea. I'm sorry to hear that, but I'm glad the store stayed in the family. And forgive me for calling your grandpa grumpy." Christian spoke kindly, his honesty written all over that handsome face.

My boss chuckled. "No, don't apologize. Grandpa was an old grump. But he was also a fluffy marshmallow on the inside. He wanted to make sure that I would be okay when he passed, so he left me the store that I grew up in. It's a nice circle of life, I think. Looking around, I can feel him here. It's comforting. Plus, it's what I know, right?"

Cecil rang up their books while he chatted, practically pushing me out from behind the register after they'd paid. "Now, go have lunch with these nice guys! I've got it covered here. I better not see you back too soon either!"

"We'll have him back in an hour, Cecil. It was nice to meet you, by the way." Christian said as he guided me out the door, his palm resting lightly between my shoulder blades.

When we got outside, he pointed me toward a little cafe across the street. It was another cute little spot, in an overly cute little town. Kent took all of their books and said: "I'm going to leave you guys to it. I need to get back to the shop, we have a big order going out this afternoon and I've been gone too long as it is."

Without giving us time to argue, he turned and rushed off in the opposite direction. Christian just smiled easily and guided us on toward the cafe. "Well, it's Kent's loss. This place makes an awesome French dip sandwich. If you like roast beef, you'll love it."

Before I barely processed what was happening, we were in the cafe and seated across from each other in a small two-person booth. A heavily pregnant omega came over to drop off menus and get our drink orders. I eyed his stomach, thinking ahead and wondering how I would ever accommodate a belly that large. I looked down at my own small bump with more than a little trepidation.

"Liam? Did you know what you'd like to drink?" I jerked my head up at Christian's voice. I quickly ordered apple juice, embarrassed at having gotten distracted while the server was waiting.

The other omega just grinned. "I'm Billy. And don't worry about getting spacey. It's part of the whole pregnancy thing. Might as well get your alpha here used to it now, while you're still in the first trimester. It only gets worse from here, trust me."

I opened my mouth to deny that Christian was my alpha, but he was already chuckling and saying: "Thanks for the heads up, Billy. It's good information to know."

After Billy left, Christian apologized quietly. "I'm sorry

if I overstepped, Liam. Especially on our first date. I just figured that you probably didn't want to air your business. Who cares if people assume that's my kid in there? I don't mind."

My mind was spinning all over the place when he said that. The first thing that popped out of my mouth though? "This is a date?"

Christian smiled shyly and glanced down at his hands that were folded in front of him on the table. "It can be. I mean, I don't want to interfere with things if you're involved though." He looked up with eyes full of questions that he was too polite to ask.

I sighed softly. "No, I'm not involved with anyone. We broke up long before I found out I was pregnant actually. It's a long depressing story, but I'm on my own now."

Christian looked at me in confusion. "Your alpha wasn't the one who," he broke off and gestured vaguely at my still bruised face. He seemed unsure how to politely mention my obvious signs of assault.

Billy came over with our drinks and pulled out his order pad. Relieved for the brief reprieve to gather my thoughts, I told him that I wanted to try the French dip that Christian had suggested. After Christian ordered the same, Billy took off again. I looked over at the kind alpha and took a deep breath. Okay. I could do this.

"I don't think we have time for the long story, so I'll just give you the condensed version."

Christian reached across the table for my hand. "You don't have to tell me anything, Liam. It's not my business, really. I'm sorry if I put you on the spot."

I shook my head. "No, you've been kind. But, it will feel good to let someone know anyway, I suppose. I'm not from here, obviously. I just got here the day that you met me. So, yeah, Gene and I broke up three months ago after he forced himself on me while I was asleep. We were dating, but still. We didn't live together, but he had a key. Gene had been out drinking and decided to just come and make use of me. After he left, I called the cops. They didn't do more than give him a slap on the wrist. Apparently just being an omega meant that I was asking for it. And alphas can't be expected to control their urges around us teasing omegas, or so they said."

Christian's eyes narrowed as he asked through gritted teeth. "And how were you supposedly teasing him by being asleep while locked inside your own home?"

I shrugged. "By existing? I don't know. The cops in that town were all a bunch of good ol' boys and my ex is the son of the mayor. I didn't have a chance against him, but I had to try. I at least wanted it on record, you know?"

He nodded, his hold tightening on my hand. It was comforting, actually. Continuing, I said: "I didn't even know I was pregnant for a long time. Then I got really sick for a few weeks, couldn't hold anything down. When I went to the doctor, they ran a pregnancy test. I didn't tell Gene. I wasn't sure yet if I even wanted to, to be honest. I mean, yeah, it's his kid. But he kind of lost the right to it when he forced himself on me."

I stopped to take a drink of juice, so I could get the rest out. "So, earlier last week he showed up at my apartment. I didn't want to let him in, but he pushed his way past me when I stupidly opened the door. His friend's sister worked at the clinic, and word had gotten to him. He demanded that I have an abortion because I was supposedly a lying omega that had tried to have him arrested. When I refused, he beat me up. He even kicked me in the stomach, in an attempt to make me lose the baby."

Christian had tears in his eyes as I stoically shared my nightmare. "He left me there, and I woke up in the hospital the next day. A neighbor had called it in. When I heard Gene's voice in the hall asking for me, I ran away dressed in my hospital gown."

I smiled sadly at the memory. It was probably really funny in another context, for a twinky omega to be running from the hospital with his ass swinging in the breeze. "I hid out until dark, then went to my apartment long enough to get dressed and grab my wallet. I left everything else behind and hitched a ride out of town. I spent the next two days hitching rides across three states in an effort to put as much distance between us as possible. My last ride dropped me here, and now here we are."

Christian's head slowly swiveled from side to side as he looked at me with respect. "That's an incredible story, Liam. I can't believe that you endured all that and now just a week later, you're sitting here with me. You're starting over in a strange place, and you're pregnant? And with no support system? That's crazy. I don't want to pressure you after what that Gene prick put you through, but I want you to know that I want to be your friend. I can be there for you, Liam. My dad was a single omega with two kids from two different alpha-holes that took off before they even met us. I know what you're in for, from watching my dad."

I smiled at him, turning my hand in his to grasp it. "I appreciate that, Christian. I don't know that I'm ready for more than a lunch date right now, but I'm definitely going to take you up on that offer of friendship regardless."

Christian smiled with relief. "Thank you. I was afraid that I sounded like a creeper, putting that out there like that. Especially with you being pregnant. I'm sure your primary concern is to protect your child right now, not worrying about alphas and their flirtations."

Billy came up right then with our food, and I reluctantly pulled my hand away to eat. The huge sandwich looked and smelled like heaven. My mouth watered as I looked at it and the big pile of thick steak fries that were served along with it.

I surprised everyone but Billy when I asked if I could get a side of chocolate sauce. I didn't even think about how weird it sounded until it was coming out of my mouth. Billy just winked and went off to get it.

The rest of our lunch was pleasant now that my dark story had been told. If anything, I felt a strange sense of relief to not be carrying that secret on my shoulders anymore. Christian looked amused as I dipped my fries in the chocolate, although not so much when I did the same with both of our pickle spears. I just shrugged and happily ate my fill.

After lunch, Christian took care of the bill and walked me back over to Second Chances. He gave me a short hug at the door. "Promise you'll let me know if you need me for anything?"

He looked serious, so I nodded quickly, with no intentions of following through. Lunch had been a pleasant break from my troubles, but I had no place in this sunny man's life. And he didn't need a used omega and another man's kid complicating his life, no matter what he thought.

Reluctantly, he said good-bye and walked back in the

direction of his garage. I smiled after him wistfully. If only I'd met him first, and this was his baby. How different my life would be! Shaking off my silly fantasy, I turned and went inside. Time for work. I had money to earn and a baby to support in just a few short months.

CHAPTER 5

CHRISTIAN

Days went by without any further sightings of Liam. I assumed that he was settling into his new home here in Hollydale and adjusting to the new job. There were a few times when I considered going to the store under some pretext or other, but I didn't want to force myself on him. He'd had enough of pushy alphas to last a lifetime.

I'd smelled his cinnamon scent so many times over the past week, that I was pretty much sure at this point that it was all in my head. I must associate this alley with Liam because this is where I'd met him, that had to be it.

Except, I never smelled it at lunch time. Early in the morning when I went in to open the shop, and on my way to meet Kent after work at night. That made no sense though. The only thing out here were locked doors to the various businesses that backed onto this alley, and the row of shiny white dumpsters that serviced them all.

Thanksgiving morning found me and Kent at Milo and Rafe's place. Tom was in rare form, flirting with Ian, an alpha friend of Rafe's. If I remembered right, they'd been dating a couple Christmases ago when I'd first met the pair. I had no idea what had happened there. But Kent had told me when I'd asked that he rarely saw Ian around Sweet Ballz.

Milo and Rafe were a great couple, and Milo was a good boss to my brother. Their toddler, Artie, was completely adorable. He was sitting in his booster seat playing with a red croquet ball. When I commented on it, Rafe and Milo had exchanged a secret smile while Tom suddenly chugged his glass of wine and reached for a refill.

I had no idea what that was about and was pretty sure I didn't want to know. After dinner, Ian had taken off after giving a long hug to Tom and whispering something in his ear that had Tom giggling.

Kent and I just exchanged amused glances while Milo packed a bag for Artie. The church was providing childcare for the volunteers, and they had surprisingly been happy to do that with their son. I didn't know Rafe well, but I'd assumed that someone of his obvious wealth would be above leaving his son in a daycare at a local church. Then I realized that I was being an asshole, to judge him like that.

We got to the church a little early, but they put us right to work. I was surprised by the line of people already waiting that wrapped around the building. Tom, Kent and I all got right to work while Milo and Rafe quickly went to check their little guy into childcare before coming back to meet us.

The kitchen was filled with people expertly cooking different parts of the meal, while others carved at least a dozen large turkeys. Still others were filling large aluminum pans with the various hot food and setting them up along the long row of tables that we would be lined up behind while filling plates for the different people coming in for the dinner.

They put Rafe and me to work lifting and setting up heavy folding tables, while Tom helped the group of people who were setting up row after row of folding chairs. Once Rafe and I had all the tables set up in the huge reception hall, we helped them set out the remaining chairs. Milo and Kent had pushed their way into the dessert area and could be heard shouting out orders to the other workers in their area. I smiled to myself, because Kent was only bossy like that when it came to food. He was passionate in the kitchen.

The church pastor, Reverend Ray as he'd introduced himself, explained that we would be serving dinner in a couple of shifts. Again, I was struck by how many needy people were in this town. As I thought about it, I wondered how many people in my daily life had their basic needs going unfulfilled.

It was staggering to realize that our peachy little town wasn't as perfect as it seemed at face value. I wondered if it had always been this way, and maybe our dad had sheltered us more than I'd known. The idea of that humbled me more than I wanted to admit.

After we got everything set up, we were moved into serving food. The kitchen staff was still busily cooking for the next shift of diners. Rafe, Tom, and I were all in line next to each other at the end of the long row of servers who were dishing out food. When the doors were opened, the first flood of people poured in and formed a single line. They were given a large paper platter-style plate, a napkin with plastic cutlery inside, and a small plate for dessert. The drinks were served at a separate station that they could visit after receiving their dinner.

It was heartbreaking to see the hunger in so many children's faces, and the delight in their eyes when they saw all the food. The end where we were stationed was the dessert portion. I got to dish out two different fruit salads. One with gelatin and tiny marshmallows, and one that was just fresh fruit, cubed and mixed together.

Rafe was in charge of pie. Apple, pumpkin, or pecan. Tom had cake slices and cookies to pass out. And were those fudge balls? Nope. I recognized those. I smiled when I saw the large tray of PBF Bombz from the shop set out in front of Tom.

I didn't know that the guys had donated a large amount of those for the dinner, but it didn't surprise me a bit. Now I understood why my brother had worked late the past few days. He should have told me, the jerk. I would have loved to help.

We were soon trucking along in a good rhythm, serving each person as efficiently as we could while smiling and making them feel welcomed at the same time. I noticed that all of us gave extra-large servings to the kids.

I was wistfully watching a family with a single omega dad and two little boys, one about ten and the other about four or five. A pang struck my chest that made me think of our dad and that long-ago meal in this very church, when I smelled him. Cinnamon! My head jerked up, and there he was. Liam stood with Otis of all people, with just a few people in line ahead of them.

My heart rate had calmed a little by the time they reached me, and I was able to easily greet them both. "Hey, Otis. I haven't seen you around. And Liam," I stopped and smiled gently. "I've missed you. Have you been okay? I haven't heard from you."

"Hey, sonny boy." Otis peered down at the food in front of me. "Nope. Sorry, sonny boy. I get to enjoy stuff like this way too seldom to waste myself on fruit. I'm just gonna mosey on to the good stuff while you two catch up." He winked and moved on to Rafe, leaving me facing a mortified Liam.

Needing to put him at ease, I rushed through my own story. "I'm really glad to see you, Liam. It's a little surreal to be on this side of the table, actually. The best Thanksgiving memory I have is from the year that my dad brought Kent and me here for dinner. He'd missed the charity box from the pantry that year, because he'd been working a double at the cafe. So, we ended up here."

Liam beamed. "The cafe where we had lunch? Your dad worked there?"

I nodded. "There's a reason that I'm partial to their French dip. I've eaten everything on the menu at some point or other. My dad worked there for over a decade. I stand by that French dip though. Best I've ever had."

Liam smiled and held out his plate finally. "Could I get a little of each? I've been really craving fruit."

Otis' plate shot out from the side. "Here, boy. Pile some on mine too, Liam's plate is fuller than mine. Let's make sure he gets plenty for that little girl in there."

My eyebrows shot up but Liam just shrugged. "Otis swears that I'm carrying a girl and that he is never wrong. I figure the odds of him being right are 50/50, so why argue?"

I grinned and put a fat spoonful of cubed fruit on Otis'

plate and a large serving of the sweet one with marsh-mallows on Liam's. He had to move on then, the line was still long behind him. I smiled softly and said: "Happy Thanksgiving, Liam. I hope this turns out to be one of your best Thanksgiving memories like it was for me."

Liam blushed and said shyly: "It already has, Christian. Happy Thanksgiving." Then he moved along and I had to turn to the next person in line. The rest of the line was a blur of faces. When another alpha came to replace me for a short break, I looked around for Liam and Otis. But they were already gone. I was bummed to miss them, but glad that they'd come.

I felt stupid for not realizing that Liam wouldn't have a place to go for Thanksgiving, or that he'd be in need. But the more I thought about it, of course he was poor. The guy had fled an abusive situation with the shirt on his back. He'd just barely started working in a thrift store! Damn. Now I was getting concerned and wondering if he even had a decent place to live.

I decided that finding out would be my next mission. And if he needed my help, providing it would be the following mission. Whether he liked it or not, I was determined to do what I could for the man.

CHAPTER 6

LIAM

I was tossing and turning, unable to get warm while also sweating like crazy. Sitting up, I tried to cough, but even though my lungs were rattling and wheezing, nothing was coming up. I flopped back down on my pillow, my mind going back to the previous week and the best holiday ever.

Dinner had been a surprise on Thanksgiving, to find Christian and Tom there serving. I hadn't known what to do with myself that day, with everything in town shut up tight. I had planned to make do on the crackers and peanut butter that I carried in my backpack, but Otis had done one of his surprise appearances when I was pulling my sleeping bag and pillow out from behind the bush where I hid them during the day.

I'd turned around with the plan to lay them out and take a nap after eating my fill of crackers. I nearly screamed when I'd turned to find Otis sitting on the curb behind me. I dropped everything and plopped down next to him.

"Otis! You've got to quit scaring me like that! You do get that I'm pregnant, right? It's just not cool to freak out the pregnant dude, man!"

He had just laughed and shoved his ever-present stogie into the inner pocket of the weathered leather jacket he always wore. "Sorry, kiddo. I'll work on making noise the next time I drop in. Now listen, put that shit back away and come with me. We've got us a hot date for dinner at the church down the way. They put out a nice spread every year for Thanksgiving. All are welcome, and there's plenty of food. Come on, kiddo. Don't disappoint an old man."

I'd just shaken my head and shoved everything back away. I hesitantly left my backpack there too, crossing my fingers that it would be okay. It should be. As far as I could tell, only Otis and I knew about this place. I didn't mind going to the church dinner. My old town had done similar things for the needy. Only then, I'd been on the other side of the table, ladling out mashed potatoes with a smile. I shook my head at the irony of fate and pushed myself up to go with Otis.

I walked everywhere I went in this town. And since every place I wanted or needed to go was in the same small two or three block radius, it was fine. I'd been smart enough to have picked a good pair of shoes when I'd fled my apartment, a fact I thanked my lucky stars for every day. There was a long line winding around the building, which didn't surprise me. Even cute little towns like this had their underbelly of poverty. Most citizens just didn't see it.

Otis wisecracked our way through the wait, making me feel like I was actually spending the holiday with a beloved friend or family member. The big shock was when I'd reached the end of the line of tables and seen Christian standing there serving food. It wasn't that it was a surprise to see the kind alpha doing something like this. Heck, I'd done it myself.

It was just that I hadn't expected to see him and it caught me off guard. Not Otis though. The big stinker was definitely not surprised, despite how he'd tried to pretend otherwise. That twinkle in his eye gave him away every time.

I couldn't find it in myself to be upset though. Seeing Christian made my day complete in some odd way. Otis and I had shared a nice meal before he'd walked me "home" again. I'd wanted to say good-bye to my alpha friend, but he was busy.

Turning over now, I fought off another fruitless cough and tried to get warm. My teeth were chattering while sweat poured off me. Before I could process anything more, the world got fuzzy and I passed out cold. When I woke up, it was cold and dark while the world moved around me in a weird whirl.

My vision was blurry, but I could smell crisp, tart apples. I became alert enough to realize that I was being carried by a pair of strong arms that were attached to that delicious smell. In the back of my mind, I heard a familiar voice soothing me in a gruff rasp: "It's okay, kiddo. Let sonny boy here get you some help. Don't worry, you and your girl will be just fine."

I wasn't sure whose voice that was right now or why it made me feel so peaceful, but I just curled up against the hard chest that smelled so good and let the darkness pull me under.

I woke up from the weird dream I'd been having of rolling around in an apple orchard, to find myself in a hospital bed with an IV sticking out of my arm. That dream had been so real, that I could still smell the tart apple scent. Blinking my eyes, I looked around the room. Oh. No wonder I smelled apples. Christian was here.

Wait. Christian was here? Why? And how did I get here? My brain raced as I looked over at the haggard looking alpha who was currently slouched in the small, hard plastic chair that was sitting next to my bed. He was unshaven and had dark circles under his eyes.

The poor alpha looked so uncomfortable. His legs were bent at the knees, ankles crossed. Those muscular arms strained at the fabric of the snug black t-shirt he wore, his arms crossed over his chest, hands tucked into his armpits. His neck was strained to the side, his mouth lolling open with a cute little line of drool dripping from the corner.

"Look who's awake! Let me take your vitals, and then I'll call your doctor in." I looked up to see a cheerful nurse with a friendly smile. She began an efficient check of my temperature, blood pressure, and oxygen saturation levels. Ripping off the blood pressure cuff with a loud rip of velcro, she made notes on a clipboard that was attached to the foot of my bed.

She moved a bed tray table closer to my bed. "There's a full pitcher of fresh ice water for you, I just put it in here a little while before you woke up. The cup is full too, drink up. You need the fluids, hon." With a brisk nod, she turned to leave but stopped and looked back at me with a gentle smile. "I'll call Dr. Samuels now, then we'll see if we can start feeding you soon. It's good to see you awake."

I felt eyes on me and turned to see Christian staring at me wondrously. "You woke up! Oh, Liam. What a relief! I've been scared out of my fucking mind. Forgive my French."

I stretched a shaky hand out for the water while I rasped: "That's not French. I took it in high school. I'm pretty sure that fucking isn't a French word, alpha."

Christian grinned as he stood and lifted the cup for me. He turned the bendy straw toward my lips. I took a grateful pull on the straw, almost moaning with delight as the cool liquid washed over my parched throat. When I pushed the straw away, he set the cup back down. Pulling his chair closer, he sat down and reached for my hand.

"Liam. You scared the crap out of me. What happened to your promise to come to me if you needed anything?" His eyes were filled with concern as he held my hand and sat patiently waiting for my response.

"I didn't want to be a bother." I tried to look away but couldn't resist the pull of those brown eyes. "Honest. I wasn't feeling great, but I didn't know that I was hospital level sick. I would've come for help because of the baby, if not myself."

He shook his head, tears filling his eyes. "I'm not talking about your illness, although we'll come back to that. I'm talking about where I found you. And don't tell me it was a one-time thing, because now I understand why I've been smelling cinnamon every day. Except at lunch, but that's when you're at work. I feel like an idiot for not realizing that you had nowhere to go."

I bit my lip, blushing with mortification that this gorgeous, kind alpha had found me sleeping behind a bunch of dumpsters like a stray dog.

"Hey, now. None of that. You did the best you could

with what you had. But, Liam. That's over. I'm sorry, but even if you don't want to accept me as your alpha, I'm still your friend."

"I never said that I didn't want to accept you. I believe my exact words at lunch were that I didn't know if I was ready for more than a lunch date. Yet. Not that I didn't want more, but I can't do that to you. I just don't think that you deserve to be stuck with someone else's kid, Christian. I wish I'd met you first, but that's not what happened."

Christian reached out a single finger and wiped away the tear that was rolling down my cheek. "Why don't you let me worry about what I deserve having in my life? And Liam? The bigger question in my mind is if I deserve the honor of having a guy like you in my life. You're special, Liam. I can't explain it, but I'm pulled toward you. Look at how we met, literally running into each other? Talk about a magnetic pull, right? Now I want you to know my thoughts on your baby. Having a child, whether it's mine biologically or not, isn't something I would ever consider myself stuck with. It would be a privilege, not a curse."

I looked into his sincere face curiously. "Why do I think that you've been giving this some thought? How long have you been thinking of this, Christian?"

"Honestly? It's pretty much been in my mind since we met, as stalkerish as that probably makes me sound. But definitely for the past two and a half days that I've been watching you deliriously fight for consciousness."

"Wait, I've been here for over two days?" I asked with shocked horror.

A deep voice came from the doorway. "You certainly have, Mr. Leigh. You were critically ill, I would say. You're lucky that Mr. Hawkins found you when he did, things could have been so much worse for both you and your child."

I turned my head to see a tall, lanky alpha striding into the room, his white doctor's coat flapping against his legs with each step. He had a head full of jet black hair and sparkling blue eyes. I would say he was handsome, except that no alpha compared to the man sitting at my side.

"Welcome back to the land of the living, Mr. Leigh. I'm Dr. Samuels. Now let's get you up so I can take a listen to those lungs of yours."

Obediently, I submitted to his examination. Once he was finished, he rolled over a stool and took a seat while he made notes on my chart. "I'm certain that you have many questions, Mr. Leigh. Let me just start with the big ones. Your baby is fine, first and foremost. Those little ones are pretty hardy there in the womb, you'd be surprised." He clicked his pen shut and stuck it in his pocket.

"You came in with a severe case of pneumonia with a

high fever. We have you on a heavy dosage of antibiotics. You are already doing much better, but a lot of that is due to the fever coming down and getting your body hydrated. We can release you tomorrow if your vitals remain steady, as long as I know you have someone to take care of you. You're going to be weak for a few weeks due to decreased lung capacity. Not to mention that you were dehydrated and malnourished. You need to take better care of yourself, Mr. Leigh. If you're not strong, you'll be in trouble when that baby comes."

"Don't worry, Doc. I've got the care taking part handled as soon as you decide that he is well enough to leave." Christian spoke firmly, his jaw set with eyes that dared me to disagree.

I nodded, trying to hide the shiver of delight that ran through my body as he took charge of me as though he were already my alpha.

Dr. Samuels had a few more things to go over with us before excusing himself with the promise to have the nurse order me a tray of food. Christian looked over at me shyly then. "I hope I didn't overstep by saying that to the doctor. But, Liam, you're coming home with me. I'm not letting you spend another night out with the trash. That's not happening. Not ever again."

Reluctantly, I nodded my agreement. "It's not like I have many options, so I'll accept your offer. But as soon as I'm on my feet, I'll start looking for a place."

"Hey, Liam? It wasn't an offer, babe. That was me being assertive. I didn't want to push you before, but now I'm afraid I'm going to have to be pushy so that I can take care of you. Do you have any idea how much it killed me when I found you there like that? Curled up like a stray cat? No, babe. You deserve so much better than that. If I'm not enough for you, then you can go on your way once you have enough saved to support yourself and the baby. Until then, I'm going to bunk with Kent and you'll have my room. It will be perfectly fine, you'll see."

"Wait. Kent lives there too?" I suddenly felt a lot better, knowing that we wouldn't be all alone. It wasn't that I didn't trust him. I just wanted to take this slowly. I had a feeling this was going to matter.

"Yes, Kent lives there too. You'll be safe. And no, you won't be in our way. I promise."

We stared at each other for a long moment. Blowing out a sigh, I finally agreed. "Okay. But if it gets to be too much, can you just promise that you'll tell me?"

Christian raised the back of my hand and bent to kiss it. "I promise that you will never be too much. But if things get hard, I promise to discuss it with you and try to reach for a compromise. Is that a good enough promise?"

I grinned and shook my head. "Okay. Good enough,

alpha. You win. Congratulations, you now have a sick house guest to look after."

Christian rubbed a thumb across my knuckles and said softly: "No, I have my future mate to look after. And I will treasure every moment." He stood then and pulled his hand back as a nurse came in carrying a tray of food. "I'm going to step out while you eat, I have a few important phone calls to make. I'll be back soon." With a quick brush of his lips against my cheek he was gone. I held my hand to my face, barely aware of the nurse as my brain tried to make sense of what had just happened.

CHAPTER 7

CHRISTIAN

I walked out into the hallway, my heart racing. Had I really just gone all alpha in there and all but demanded that Liam come home with me as a perspective mate? And had he actually agreed? Holy fuckballs. I hadn't been able to breathe for nearly three days. I'd alternately stood, sat, and paced beside his bed while he'd gone back and forth between complete unconsciousness and febrile delirium.

That night I'd found him I'd just gone to sleep when I heard Otis' voice in my ear. "Get up, sonny boy. Hurry now. Our Liam needs ya. He's out in the alley where you met. Follow your nose and your eyeballs. You'll see a sign that will help you find him. Go on, get moving."

I'd opened my eyes and sat up, heart racing from the strange dream like experience. Right before I laid back down, I noticed another one of those odd feathers on the floor by my bed and the faint hint of cigar smoke.

Deciding to take a chance that this wasn't just a weird dream, I'd followed the pull in my gut that commanded I obey dream Otis' voice. I'd dressed as fast as I could, stopping long enough to shove my wallet and cell phone in my pocket before flying out the door with Kent's sleep heavy voice calling my name.

I'd run the block and a half that we lived from work and gone back to the alley. Sure enough, the smell of cinnamon was strong. I'd spun around looking everywhere but up as I tried to figure out what sign it was that I was supposed to find. Finally, I'd seen a feather! It was laying in front of the row of dumpsters. When I'd walked over to get it, the cinnamon smell grew stronger.

Another feather lay beside the dumpster back by the wall. I'd walked back to get it, and that's when I realized that there was a narrow alley that formed a protective barrier between the cement wall and the row of dumpsters. The clouds moved just enough right at that moment, that a strong glow fell over the passageway with a soft light that showed me a bundle of something up against the wall near a large bush.

In a daze, I'd stumbled over there and looked down to see a small omega lying huddled in a sleeping bag right there on the ground. It was Liam! Now that I was closer, I could smell that his cinnamon scent was mixed with the cloying smell of sickness. He was coated in sweat and barely breathing, a strange rattling noise came with every inhalation. I'd tried to wake him, but he'd been too out of it to respond.

There was a backpack there next to him. I'd flung it over my shoulder and dug my phone out and called 911. I didn't tell them anything more than I had an unconscious man that I'd found collapsed behind my place of work.

Nobody but me need ever know where I'd found him. That was his story to tell. Or not. Then I'd scooped his seemingly weightless body up against my chest and carried him out of there. I'd waited at the entrance to the alley until help arrived.

That had been the beginning of nearly three days in hell. All I'd had to tell the hospital was that he was my omega and pregnant with our child. They hadn't refused me access once I'd told that whopper. I'd called Kent and told him what was happening.

The next morning I'd called Cecil and let him know. Over the past few days, Tom, Cecil, and Kent had all been in and out to check on Liam and offer me support. They all knew that I was in full on alpha mode, I suppose my affection for the omega hadn't been very secretive.

Now that he was awake, I fumbled with my phone to call Kent and give him the good news. He already knew my plan to bring Liam home, and had given his blessing. It wasn't nearly as sudden an idea as Liam might think. When I'd seen the omega that haunted my heart laying there behind the dumpsters like that, I had vowed to do whatever it took to make him mine. I wanted to protect him from ever being hurt again.

After I spoke to Kent with a crowing Tom in the background, I'd headed back to my omega's room. I heard voices before I walked in and turned the corner to find Otis standing there. I stopped and stared. How the hell had he gotten in here without me seeing him? I'd been right out in the hall on the phone. I totally would have seen him go by, right?

Shaking my head, I walked in as Otis glanced up with that familiar grin on his wrinkled face. "Hey, sonny boy. Ya did good, getting our Liam here to get help. I can only do so much, ya know?"

Moving my jaw from side to side, I carded a hand through my hair and gazed at the geezer speculatively. "No, Otis. I don't know. Why don't you tell me, old timer? I have a few questions for you right about now anyway."

Otis winked over at me. "They always do, sonny boy. Now come on over here and take a load off. You look half dead yourself." He looked back down at Liam. "Alphas, right? They never know how to take care of themselves. But then, maybe that's why every good alpha has an omega at his side."

Liam blushed and look down at his lap, his hands

moving to cover his small bump. I moved around and sat down on the hard chair that probably held my butt imprint by now. I could see both men clearly from this vantage point.

Otis leaned over and patted Liam on the shoulder. "You'll be okay now, kiddo. The hard times are behind ya, if you'll just trust your heart. Don't be scared to give sonny boy here a chance. Life's too short to let fear hold you back, kiddo. Trust me on that one. Now I gotta go, I got places ta be. I took the liberty of removing everything from the alley, you don't need ta go back there. Ya hear me?"

With a quick nod, Liam looked up and smiled tremulously at Otis. "Why does this feel like you're saying good-bye, Otis? Will I see you again?"

"Don't worry, kiddo. I'll be around." He winked again, with a smile for both of us. "I've got my eye on you two. You're good kids, you'll be just fine. But I'm sure I'll be popping up again if you need a little help from a frail old man."

Liam and I exchanged a smile. Otis was far from a frail old man. Hell, he could probably run circles around half the guys I know. Well, if he still had the lung power after sucking on those stogies for who knows how many years. I looked back up to thank Otis, but the dodgy bastard had taken off again.

I looked back at Liam. "Does he do that all the time to

you too? Appearing and disappearing without warning?"

Liam nodded. "And scaring the crap out of you pretty much every time? Yeah. It's kind of his thing. I didn't know that you two knew each other though? I mean, aside from when we saw you at Thanksgiving."

"Yeah, actually now that I think of it, I met you both on the same day. I've never seen him around here before that. Huh. That's something to think about. Nothing interesting ever happens here, and then I manage to meet the two of you on the same day. What a coincidence."

He looked at me with a curiously bright light in his eyes. "This makes me think of an article I saw online a few months ago. Have you ever heard of Synchronicity? The belief that there are no coincidences, just a series of seemingly unrelated events and experiences that lead us to our destiny? This whole time I've spent in Hollydale really makes me want to be a believer."

Liam yawned then, leaning back into his pillow as he smiled shyly at me. "Were you serious earlier, Christian? Do you really want me to consider having you as my alpha?"

I nodded firmly. "I can't think of anything I want more, Liam. But I also don't want you to feel indebted to me for simple human kindness. Choose me because you like me. Or because I make you smile. Or," I shrugged and wiggled my eyebrows, "maybe even because you think I'm super smexy. Just don't choose me because you think that you have to, okay?"

Liam smiled softly. "Oh, Christian. The problem is that I might just want you for all of the above reasons. But not because I think I have to, but more because I can't stand the thought of saying no and not having you in my life. Otis was right. I don't want to let fear keep me from taking a chance at happiness. For both of our sake."

CHAPTER 8

LIAM

I looked around the simple, neat bedroom that Christian had shown me. I set my backpack on the straight backed wooden chair that sat just inside the door under the light switch. Beside it was a basic black six drawer dresser, low and wide with three drawers on each side. A narrow rectangular mirror poked up from the center.

The bed was a queen-size with a plain black headboard that matched the dresser. It was made up with a simple pale blue comforter and matching sheets with two pillows plumped against the top of the bed. Two black nightstands stood on either side of the bed. Aside from a single portrait of a smiling omega and two young boys, there were no other furnishings in the room. Even the window was only dressed with a basic set of blinds. This was definitely the room of an unmated alpha.

Despite the lack of personality and layers of comforting

design elements, it smelled like home. It smelled like Christian. It smelled like safety. So yeah, home. I turned to where Christian was standing behind me. He smiled shyly with a rare look of insecurity in his eyes.

Ignoring my normal hesitation, I flung myself at him and wrapped my arms around his waist with a big hug. His hands automatically came up around my shoulders as he hugged me back. I stood there against him for as long as I could without being weird, just inhaling his scent and leaning on his strength.

Breaking the hug, I pulled back and beamed up at him. "In case you missed it any of the 537 times that I already said it, thank you so much for having me. And for giving up your bed for me. I can't believe how sweet you are to make that sacrifice."

Kent's head popped up in the doorway behind his brother's shoulder. "Don't thank him, I'm the one that has to put up with this guy's snoring again."

Christian blushed red and muttered: "I don't snore."

Kent nodded at me and said: "Yeah, actually he does. Don't say I didn't warn you in the future. But yeah, don't sweat it. It's going to be nice to have an omega around here again. We've been kinda lost since dad died." His eyes looked a little bleak as he took in the room behind me.

I looked up at Christian questioningly. He nodded. "This was my dad's room originally. I took it over a few months after he passed. We figured it was stupid to keep sharing our childhood bedroom when there was a perfectly good room standing unused." He sighed and turned, shoving his brother back playfully. "Now quit lying to my omega. You know damn well that you're the one who snores."

My heart swelled at his words. *My omega.* Lord, help me but I liked hearing that from him. I grinned though when Kent leaned over and whispered loudly: "He's totally the snorer though. Just saying." It was funny, even the idea of him snoring was cute to me. Crap. I was so screwed over this alpha and we weren't even officially together.

━━━

"Christian. I will be fine. You've taken an entire week off work now, and who knows how many days while I was in the hospital. Just go to work tomorrow and trust me to call you if I feel weak." He hadn't left the apartment once since I'd gotten out of the hospital.

Every time I coughed, he was right there to check on me and offer a drink of water. Medicine was dispensed right on time, along with vitamins and enough citrus fruit to cure scurvy for a whole boatload of pirates. It was sweet, it was adorable, it was...on my last fricken' nerve.

"Fine." He bit his lip as he looked at me with an

assessing gaze. He huffed out a sigh and said: "You're right. I need to go in tomorrow and see what's happening. One of my mechanics is running the day to day stuff, but Tim can't do payroll or banking. I need to get in there and handle business."

"See? You have a business, Christian. Don't let my being here distract you. And, I know I didn't give you a lot of reason to trust me to call on you before. But things are different now. I promise that I'll call you if I need anything at all."

I held up the cell phone that he'd insisted on giving me when I came here. He wanted me to be able to reach him anytime, day or night. But so far, he'd been within whisper distance 24/7. Or so it seemed. I kind of felt like an asshole for needing a little space, but this was the first time I'd lived with anyone in about five years.

Before that, I'd only ever lived with my parents. But on my 18th birthday, they'd disowned me after I'd refused the arranged mating they tried to push on me with the troglodyte son of my dad's boss. Apparently, keeping the boss happy was more important than their own son's future.

I'd had a small inheritance from my grandmother that got me into my little apartment. I'd worked two jobs to keep it, but I'd been happy alone in my little nest.

I wanted to be here with the Hawkins brothers, especially Christian. I just wanted a little quiet time to reflect and catch my breath.

So much had happened in the past few weeks, my head spun just thinking about it. I was still recovering from the pneumonia, although I felt stronger every day. From what Dr. Samuels had said, I still had another couple weeks of recovery before I could think of going back to work. Cecil had been sweet about it though, telling me that my job was safe no matter how long it took me to get back on my feet.

Tucking the phone back into my pocket, I curled my legs up on the couch beneath me and said: "Now wasn't I promised a movie this afternoon?"

Christian grinned and picked up the remote. "Do you want to pick the movie or make the popcorn?" I snorted and hopped up with a light giggle. We both knew what happened if he made the popcorn. Yeah, burnt popcorn and squealing smoke detectors just didn't go along with movie time.

CHAPTER 9

CHRISTIAN

The morning flew by, and I found myself suddenly looking at the clock to find that I'd missed my regular lunch hour. Picking up my phone, I called Liam. While the phone rang, I second guessed myself. Maybe a text would've been better?

I knew that he was feeling a little antsy and needed some alone time. I got that. He wasn't used to living with other people. He hadn't even lived with the alpha-hole who'd sired his child. I purposely thought of the douche only as the sire, because I intended to be the child's father.

"Hello? Christian?" Liam's sweet voice came clearly across the line, strong and true. Good. He hadn't been coughing recently.

"Hey, gorgeous. I don't want to interrupt your alone time. I just wanted to see if you needed me to bring you anything before I come home tonight."

"Oh, umm, no. I'm fine actually. I was just about to make myself some lunch. Did you eat with Kent today?"

"No. Actually, I got caught up with paperwork and kinda missed lunch altogether. I should probably go grab something, I suppose." I listened to his breathing, content to have even this connection with Liam.

"Umm. If you want, you could just come here? I can make two sandwiches as easily as one, and then you're not having to buy lunch." His voice sounded hesitant, as if he expected me to say no.

"Sure you don't mind? I can be there in ten minutes if you want a little company for lunch."

"That sounds great. I'll get started on it. See you a little bit." I could hear the happy relief in his voice, which all on its own made me glad I'd called instead of texting.

"See you in a little bit." I hung up the phone and left my office, whistling all the way back to my apartment. I walked in the door right as Liam was setting two plates on the table that was already laid out with place mats, silverware, and glasses filled with iced tea. A little wedge of lemon floated on top. Blinking, I looked at the pleasant set up, then over at Liam who was sliding into the seat he'd been using next to mine.

"Wow. You did all of this in ten minutes? You're fast." I wanted to slam my head against the wall. That was the best I could come up with for a compliment? Seriously?

Liam blushed prettily though and glanced down at his plate that matched mine with a thick egg salad sandwich and a healthy serving of fruit salad. "It was a little too quiet around here today. I got bored. I decided to keep busy and found myself making all of this," his hand waved over the plates.

"No offense?" I grinned and toasted him with my glass. "But I could get used to you to being bored if it delivers a nice lunch like this one."

Liam grinned. "Wait until you see what I've got planned for dinner then."

My eyes widened, and I looked around the room to see if I could get a hint by what he had out to defrost, but nothing could be seen.

With a scoffing flicker of his fingers, Liam said: "Please. I'm an omega who had a traditional upbringing. You'll never catch me with uncooked ingredients lying about. Just trust me. Be on time and bring your appetite."

If the taste of the egg salad that was currently giving me a mouthgasm was any indicator, I was in for a fantastic dinner. "Trust me, babe. Not only will I be on time, I'll probably be ten minutes early."

Liam giggled, and we ate our lunch companionably. He

told me stories from his childhood, and I told him about my dad. It was nice to have a reason to come home for lunch, but even nicer to have a person who cared enough to put together a nice meal for just a quick lunchtime visit.

When I reluctantly rose after glancing at the clock and reached for my plate, Liam shocked me by smacking my hand. "I've got it. You go back to work, just let me do this for you."

"But babe. You're still recovering from a major illness. You don't need to overwork yourself." I tried to protest but Liam had already stood and was deftly stacking our dishes.

"Christian. I've got this, trust me. I will take a nap after I put the leftovers away and load these few things into the dishwasher." He turned imperiously and began clearing the table.

"But, my dad taught us that the ones that don't cook do the clean-up."

"And when I go back to work, that will be a good system. Right now, I'm home with lots of free time. You don't want me to rip my hair out from sheer boredom, do you?" He pouted playfully, his hand going up to run his fingers through that gorgeous, thick, shoulder length hair that I was dying to play with myself.

Wistfully pulling my eyes back from his hair, I jerked

my chin in a nod. "Fine. You win. You get to do all the work. I'll just go back to the shop and shuffle my papers around." I sighed loudly, as if I were making a giant concession.

His eyes twinkling, Liam stood up on his tiptoes and gave me a kiss on the cheek. "Enjoy the rest of your day then."

Stunned by the casual display of affection, I pressed my hand up against my cheek without thinking. I was staring at him as he chuckled and said dryly: "You might want to pick your jaw up off the floor, alpha. I haven't had a chance to mop yet."

Shaking my head, I turned to go when Liam stopped me. "Wait! I almost forgot!" I looked back to see him pulling a brown paper back from the fridge.

"I texted Kent and told him you'd be dropping off his lunch on your way back. He's expecting this," he smiled and proudly handed me a bag for my brother. I looked at the bag and back at Liam.

"You know you're spoiling us, right? We haven't eaten anything besides take-out or freezer meals since our dad died." I really wasn't kidding. My brother excelled at making sweets. This did not extend to a desire to cook other kinds of food. And since I didn't want to court Type II Diabetes, I ate sandwiches instead of Kent's cookies and delicious brownies.

Before Liam could reply or step away, I swooped down and kissed his cheek like he'd done to me. Flashing him a quick wink, I smiled at his surprised expression and ducked out the door and headed back toward work after making a quick detour to deliver lunch to my brother.

CHAPTER 10

LIAM

The weeks were flying by, and I was settled comfortably into the Hawkins brothers' world before I knew it was happening. Even though I had gone back to work now, I still made dinner every night. I only worked six hours a day, so I got home in plenty of time to get a nice dinner on the table before my boys got home.

Christian and I were *thisclose* to getting serious, while Kent had already become the brother that I'd never known I wanted. I felt badly about making the two guys share a room for the past few weeks, but I had a feeling that would be changing soon. I knew I wanted Christian to be my mate. I just wanted it to happen naturally.

Christmas was two days away, and I had the next ten days off. Cecil had closed the store down to go on the Hawaiian vacation that he apparently took every year during holidays. It was a tradition his grandfather had started, and Cecil was only too happy to continue with it.

I was just thrilled to have the time off. My feet were starting to swell, and I'd had a lot of heartburn lately. I was getting a little bigger in the belly now that I was in my fourth month. I had a doctor appointment this afternoon. I was looking forward to finding out how the baby was doing.

Aside from the awful morning sickness I'd had right before I'd discovered I was pregnant, I hadn't had many problems. There was another complication that had started to bother me in the past week, and I was hoping to remedy it soon. Maybe even tonight?

At first, I'd thought it was just the close living quarters with the man I knew would be my mate. But I'd been looking at the pregnancy website that tells us omegas what to expect during each step of our pregnancy when I'd seen a major symptom of the second trimester. Apparently, being horny was an actual symptom? Finally. Something I could get behind. Hmm. Or in front of...oh, yeah. Bent over in front of Christian would definitely solve this, er, symptom of my pregnancy.

Needing to get my mind off of my frustrated libido, I grabbed the lunches I had bagged in the fridge and left the apartment. After tapping off a quick text to Christian, I headed down to Sweet Ballz.

I'd even made a lunch for Tom, not wanting to leave him out. Tom had been making a lot of friendly overtures to me since my illness, not to mention the fact that he'd been instrumental in helping me to get my job at Second Chances.

I walked around the back side just as Christian was walking up. He greeted me with a hug, our new normal, and opened the door for me to enter ahead of him. I was surprised to see the work table clean today, with Kent and Tom sitting there waiting for me to arrive with lunch.

They even had bottles of water sitting out for the four of us. Setting the bags down, I gave Kent a side hug before moving around to hug Tom. Of course, these hugs were nothing like the close full-bodied hugs that I shared with Christian. No, his hugs were special.

"Tom is so excited to have a homemade lunch! What did Liam bring to eat?" Tom was already settled on his stool and reaching for the bag with his name on it. He squealed happily when he saw that I'd made chicken salad with little bits of chopped cranberries, grapes and pecans. It was a personal favorite of his that I'd made a few times before when I'd had time to bring lunch.

Tom excitedly dug into his sandwich while the alphas were excited to find themselves with roast beef. I'd been bored, what can I say? I nibbled at my own sandwich, while Kent pulled out the container of chopped fruit I'd brought along. It was safe to say that I was definitely craving fruit. I couldn't get enough of it, especially cantaloupe and honeydew melon. It wasn't exactly in season, but Kent had surprised me with some a few days ago. I guess it paid to be friends with food vendors.

I reached over and plucked up a big slice of honeydew, savoring the flavor. I saw the flash of lust in Christian's eyes as I licked the juice that had dribbled from the corner of my mouth with a flick of my tongue. A sudden weird urge came over me and I turned to Kent. "Do you have any melted caramel?"

He shrugged. "No, but I can melt you some in the microwave in less time than it will take you finish that sandwich." My face must have lit up from excitement because the young alpha was getting up and moving around efficiently doing just that before I even processed what he was doing. I finished my sandwich right as he was setting a small dish of melted caramel in front of me.

The three of them sat there watching in horrified fascination as I dipped the different melons into the caramel, savoring every bite. They didn't flinch when I dipped the banana or apple slices, but the pineapple slice really threw them off. I just shrugged and enjoyed my treat.

After all of us were finished, Kent cleared away our mess and began wiping down the table with cleaning spray and a dry cloth. I suddenly remembered what I'd been thinking about when I woke up this morning.

I looked over at Christian and asked: "Why don't we have a Christmas tree?"

He looked at me with a shrug. "Kent and I just haven't bothered the past few years. And then the last couple of years we've gone to his boss' place for the holiday. Why? Would you like one."

Tom and I shared shocked looks. I looked back over at Christian and bounced on my seat like a little kid. "Duh! We need a tree! This is our first holiday together, I want to decorate!"

"Well, okay then. I can bring the shop truck home tonight. We can use it to go get a tree. I'm sure there's gotta be a few decent ones left, right?"

Kent grinned at his brother. "Are you kidding? Last minute people like us are their thing. We'll get one. And we can pull out dad's ornaments! I don't know if our lights are any good though."

I shivered with excitement. "I can go shopping this afternoon while you guys finish your work day! I'll pick up whatever you think we need, and everything you don't."

Christian said practically: "Liam. You don't have a car or know your way around outside of this small area.

And you can't be carrying heavy bags of crap all around, you're pregnant. Not to mention, you're barely over that pneumonia from last month. Also, don't you have an appointment with your OB/GYN this afternoon?"

Tom's eyes lit up as he tapped his phone. "Tom just texted Milo to come in for the afternoon. Milo has been missing the store anyway. Milo is on the way. And Tom loves babies! Will Tom get to come into the exam room with Liam and hear the sweet baby heartbeat too?"

I looked at him curiously for about half a second until I realized his intentions. "You're coming with me? That's awesome, Tom! Maybe after my appointment, you can help me find some clothes too. I have a few paychecks stashed that I was saving for my own place, but..."

I looked down at the shirt stretched thin across my growing belly. "Yeah, I think I need clothes. I should have looked at Second Chances before Cecil closed down for the year." I was worried all of a sudden, afraid of how much I'd spend with Tom in tow.

Christian leaned across the table and took my hand. "You don't need to save for another place. Go get yourself some clothes, at least a week's worth of outfits, if not more. Go crazy. In fact," he pulled his hand back and pulled out his wallet. Sliding a credit card across the table, he continued. "I want to pay for it all. Go shopping, my treat. Don't you dare come back without enough clothes to wear. Get a few sizes up too, I imagine your belly is going to start getting much bigger soon."

I shook my head and went to push the card back, but Tom's hand slipped under mine and snagged the card. "Tom will make certain that Liam has an appropriate wardrobe. Luckily for Christian, Tom has a friend with a discount. Also," he shrugged, "holiday sales."

Wanting to argue, I opened my mouth but closed when I saw the determined look on my alpha's face. I bit my lip and gave a quick nod. "Okay, but I'm paying you back. And, thank you."

Christian grinned. "We'll see. Just promise that you'll go and have fun with Tom, that's all the thanks I need. And call me after you see the doctor? I just wish I could be there to hear the heartbeat again too." He paused wistfully, then added another thought. "Although, I wouldn't say no to a little fashion show later?"

Milo arrived a few minutes after that, and Tom started trying to drag me out the door. I didn't know Milo, but I was a little concerned by the alarm in his eyes when Tom excitedly told him that he was taking me out for a makeover.

Christian just grinned and gave me a hug. He whispered into my ear, "Have fun, babe. Maybe you could think about buying something sexy for that fashion show?"

Tom overheard and giggled as he dragged me out of

there. He all but shoved me into his little green car and barely waited for me to buckle up before speeding off down the road.

I had absolutely no idea what the hell I'd gotten myself into, but by the way Tom was vibrating with excitement? I was pretty sure I was in for an afternoon of death by shopping. But first, the doctor!

CHAPTER 11

CHRISTIAN

The fashion show didn't end up happening that night. Liam didn't get home until dinner time. He'd called me from the car so that Kent and I could come down and help haul everything upstairs. The poor guy looked worn out but was insistent on the tree shopping when he saw my shop truck parked in front of our building.

Tom had ended up joining us for dinner at The Glazed Bun, and then we'd gone and picked out a tree. By the time we'd made it home, I'd carried my sleeping omega upstairs while Kent carried the tree up and put it in place.

Tom stayed to help him decorate, so that Liam could wake up tomorrow on Christmas Eve and find a fully decorated tree. I was off for the next four days, since Christmas fell on a Friday this year.

When I carried Liam into his room, he woke up a little. "Christian? Close the door and stay with me for awhile?"

I carried him over and set him down on the bed. "Liam, I don't think that's a good idea, you're tired. You don't know what you're saying."

He looked more alert as he said: "Yeah, I do. I've been thinking about it all day. I probably just want to cuddle, if that's okay."

"That's more than okay. I'm just gonna go change into my pajama pants, and I'll be right back, okay?" Liam nodded, and I slipped out to go change. Tom and Kent were arguing and laughing about the proper placement of our tree, and Christmas carols were now playing in the background. I shook my head at that odd friendship and went to change my clothes.

A few minutes later, I was changed into just a pair of pajama pants. I'd left my shirt off because it was warm in the apartment, a fact that I was second guessing as I tapped on the door and let myself into Liam's room. He had the lights off, but the moonlight streaming through the partially open blinds was enough for me to see clearly in the dim room.

He sat up with an equally bare chest, pulling back the covers beside him. As I climbed in, Liam waited for me to get comfortable before laying back down with his head on my arm. "Thanks for doing this, Christian. I'm just so emotional and lonely lately."

I turned on my side facing his profile as he lay there on his back looking up at the ceiling, my arm still under his head. I put my free arm across the front of him and snuggled him close. "It's okay, Liam. We all get lonely and emotional around the holidays. And being in a new place and pregnant? I can't blame you. I'm surprised that you've held up so long, now that I think about it."

He turned and looked at me then, his eyes searching mine. "Will you kiss me? Or is that too much to ask?"

"Liam, I've only been waiting for you to give me a sign, babe." I leaned over and pressed my lips to his reverently. Taking my time, I kissed him in all the ways I'd been dreaming of for so many weeks now. I kissed his top lip, barely sucking it between mine. Then I kissed both dimples at the corners of his smile, before moving back to suck his bottom lip deeply between my lips.

He sighed happily, his entire body relaxing under mine. Tilting my head, I rubbed our lips together a few times before kissing him fully. On his gasp, I slid my tongue inside his mouth to get a taste of him. We kissed slowly, our tongues intertwining and sliding against each other. His hands came up around my neck, pulling me closer.

My arm under his head bent to pull him into my

embrace as I slowly stroked his side with my free hand, finally resting it on his hip as he rolled to face me. He had one hand rubbing against the short hair on the top of my closely cropped head, while the other rested between us now. His fingers were playing with the single patch of thick hair in the center of my chest, as he moaned into my mouth and thrust his hips against mine.

My hand slid down to cup his butt, and I froze in surprise. My eyes popped open and I pulled back, breaking our kiss. "Is that satin I feel?"

His eyes danced in the moonlight. "I may or may not have found a store that specializes in sexy paternity clothes for omegas. I decided to buy you these satin manties for Christmas. Don't worry, I bought them myself, because they are meant to be a gift." He was rambling a little now. "Is it weird though that I bought you a gift that I planned to wear?"

I looked at him blankly, unable to even begin to unpack all the words that he'd just put out there. I was stuck on one. "Manties?"

Liam giggled softly. "Man panties, or manties for short. Do you like?"

My hand was now moving again, roaming all over his small bubble butt, enjoying the feel of the smooth satin over his firm globes. I nodded eagerly. "Oh, yeah. I like. Can I turn the light on and see them better? Or is that a no right now?"

He ducked his head shyly. "Um. Maybe in the morning? I'm kind of weird about you seeing the baby bump. I'm not as toned as you are, even without the baby."

Wordlessly, I scooted down in the bed and began to kiss his belly. I pulled my hands free so that I could hold his still smallish bump and lavish my attentions on it. Liam tensed up at first, then finally began to relax again. Remembering the manties, I moved a hand down to cup his crotch while I kept pressing kisses across his belly.

His dick was a hard steel bar, the head poking up over the stretchy lace panel at the front that would accommodate his growing belly. Lifting up onto my elbow, I stretched out beside to watch his lovely moonlit face while I rubbed him off through the satiny fabric. I used my thumb to tease the tip of his leaking cock with the stretchy lace.

I gazed at him steadily while my hand kept its rhythmic pace. His eyes opened and caught mine. We were watching each other when he came, the cream shooting up onto his belly. His eyes fluttered closed as he groaned softly, his mouth falling slack while his hips jerked as he shot out the last bits of his release.

Leaning over, I licked him clean before moving back up and taking him in my arms again. After he calmed down and was breathing normal, he leaned over for another kiss. Stopping short, his lips barely touched mine as he whispered: "I really did just intend to cuddle."

I chuckled and whispered back: "Am I in trouble for going too far?"

"No, I just feel bad that I didn't return the favor."

Still whispering, I said: "Yeah, you did. If you reach down and touch my pants, you'll feel the wet spot from when I felt you through that satin and lace. By the way? Best. Gift. Ever."

Liam snickered and then kissed me softly. He pulled away and snuggled against my chest, rubbing his cheek along my pecs until he found the spot where he was most comfortable. "Christian?" He asked sleepily, a few moments later.

I yawned. "Yeah, babe?"

"Please don't leave tonight. Or ever again. Can this become our new sleeping arrangement? Or is that too weird to even ask? Please don't think I'm weird."

"Babe? It's not weird, and yeah, I'm good with this becoming our new normal. I thought you'd never ask. Good night, Liam."

"Good night, my alpha."

I smiled at the sound of that and closed my eyes. The scent of cinnamon filled my nose as I drifted off to the best sleep of my life.

The holidays were over, and it was the day before we all had to go back to work. I was sadly helping the Hawkins boys pack away their dad's precious ornaments for next year. It was an eclectic mix of old hand-blown orbs that had passed through their family, cutesy little ones that they'd picked up over the years, and ones that had been hand made from school projects.

My favorite was a little hand shaped reindeer that Christian had made when he was in kindergarten. I held up the tiny little cardboard hand and compared it to the large hands of the adult alpha. Smiling, I tucked it away carefully until next year.

My heart swelled, thinking that next year I would still be here, but we would also have a baby to spoil. Thinking about that, I asked the guys a question that had been looming on my mind. "Can I ask you guys a question?"

They both turned to look at me with matching expressions and lifted brows. "How attached are you to this apartment? I know that you lived here with your dad. Would that make it hard to move?"

Christian smiled and said: "Honestly? I think we've probably stayed here more out of habit and the easy commute than because of sentiment. Why? You want more room?"

I shrugged and rested a hand on my belly. "I think we'll need a bit more room in a few months, and I'm not exactly looking forward to carting an infant up and down those stairs either."

Kent bit his lip and said: "If it's space that's the problem, maybe I could just find a room somewhere."

I shook my head at the sweet alpha. No, he wasn't ready to live alone. I knew that before I ever lived with them. "Absolutely not, Kent. I want us to all be a family. Besides, how will Christian and I ever get alone time if the baby doesn't have Uncle Kent around?"

His face lit up in a beatific smile. "Really?" He breathed. "I'm gonna be the baby's uncle?"

Christian rolled his eyes. "Duh. Liam's my omega, and that's gonna be my baby. That makes you the uncle."

Kent frowned a little. "Then you guys need to get

married. If you're gonna be the baby's father, then you need to marry Liam. That way the baby will know you're always gonna be around. We know it, but you want everyone else to know it too. Especially the baby."

My eyes watered at the sadness in his eyes. I knew that their fathers had both peaced out of their lives early, but I hadn't realized before now the residual pain that had obviously caused for Kent. Christian seemed fine with it, but then, Kent was one of those gentler souls. As I thought about it though, it made sense. It probably made him feel unwanted. Aw, now I wanted to hug the guy.

Christian turned and walked into the bedroom. I was staring after him, wondering if it was what Kent said about the baby daddy situation or the idea of marrying me so soon that had him leaving the room. I turned and began removing ornaments again. I wasn't worried, I knew that he loved me. We hadn't had actual sex yet. We'd fooled around a lot over the past week, but so far it hadn't gone further than a few exchanged blow jobs and a lot of heavy petting.

When Kent sucked in a sharp breath, I turned to see Christian behind me on one knee. Luckily, I was holding a plastic ornament, because it dropped and bounced along the floor as I brought my hands to my mouth and stared at my alpha with tear filled eyes.

He was holding out a plain gold ring, with a hopeful smile on his face. "My idiot brother has a point, Liam. I was planning to wait until Valentine's Day to propose, but now is just as good. I know we've only known each other about two months now, so this is probably way too soon. But time doesn't matter when you know you've found the other half of your soul. I already know that I love you, babe. Will you marry me, and make me complete? Make us a family with the baby, and all the siblings we'll give the little one in the future?"

Nodding my head, I whispered: "Yes. I want to be your family. And for you to be mine. I love you too, Christian." I held out my trembling hand for him to put on the ring. He slid it onto my finger, then kissed it before standing and pulling me into his arms for a kiss. I pulled back and said firmly: "And as for future babies, Christian Hawkins? Let's get this one out of me before we plan to put another one in there."

He laughed and picked me up in his arms. Carrying me, he turned and headed to the bedroom. He stopped and looked over his shoulder at a grinning Kent. "Thanks for the push, man. Now you get to finish with taking down the tree, I need some alone time with my fiancé. And you might want to put on some music or something."

I giggled at the scandalized look on the younger alphas face as Christian spun us around and headed into our room, kicking the door closed with his foot. He carried me over to the bed and was already pulling my clothes off me before my butt even hit the mattress. Laughing, I pushed him back. "This will go a lot faster if we both strip at the same time."

He nodded quickly and left me to finish undressing while he shrugged his own clothes off. He paused when he saw me pushing down the pair of royal blue satin manties that I was wearing. His eyes glazed with lust as he watched me take them off.

I smirked and tossed them at his face. He just grinned and made a show of sniffing the crotch before tossing them over his shoulder and tackling me gently down onto the bed. While Christian was kissing my neck and working up to my ear, I asked breathlessly: "Are we really about to have our first time together while your brother is out there un-trimming the tree?"

Christian nipped at my earlobe. "Why not? He probably assumes that we've been doing this every night anyway. Trust me, this isn't weird for him. If anything, it makes him feel safe to know that we're mates now."

I pushed him back so I could focus. "Oh, man. Because now he knows I'll be staying around, so he's free to love me? Is that it?"

He nodded. "Yeah, my brother has definite abandonment issues and a romantic heart. It's a bad combo, but especially for an alpha whose dad was a douche. But, why are we talking about my brother when my dick is hard enough to cut glass? Can we circle back to him later? Please?"

I smiled and grabbed his face to pull him in for a kiss. Christian smiled against my lips and flipped us over so that I was straddling him. "I want to see you during our first time together. And I want to watch your sexy belly move while you ride me. Can you handle that?"

I shivered as I nodded at him, so excited to finally be getting here. "Supplies?" I asked quietly. His chin jerked toward the nightstand on the right side of the bed, I crawled over and opened the drawer. I pulled out a tube of lube and tossed it over beside him, before holding up the condoms with a raised brow.

"I mean, I'm good without them. I was tested a few months ago and I'm clean. I haven't been with anyone in over three years, if you want to know the ugly truth of it." He said this with more than a hint of embarrassment. I tossed the rubbers back in the drawer and closed it.

"Well, it's not like I'm going to get pregnant, and I was given a clean bill of health at the hospital as I'm sure you recall."

Crawling slowly back to straddle him again, I bit back the smug smile that wanted to come when I saw him tracking my every movement. I climbed up over his large body, straddling his hips and looking down at him happily. "You know what? I think you're kinky as heck to want our first time to be in the middle of the day with poor Kent in the next room, but I'm pretty much past caring."

In response, he silently lifted me by the hips with those muscular arms and moved me over his mouth where he could lick my rim. My head went back and I bit into a fist to keep from crying out as his tongue licked around my hole a few times before pushing its way inside. His hands were cupping my ass cheeks. I was proud to note that each one felt like a perfect handful for those large hands.

He pulled my cheeks apart and ran his tongue back and forth over every bit of flesh that he could get to, his nose rubbing against the back of my balls with each bob of his head. He pulled back and gasped: "Lube me, get me ready."

He tilted me into an awkward angle that gave him even better access to lick my hole. I was able to reach the lube and squirted a handful into my palm before tossing it back down. Reaching behind me, I gripped his long, thick cock and began stroking the lube onto it.

Once I had him nice and slippery, he pulled away from my hole with a groan. Pushing his thumbs slowly into my tight, spit-soaked pucker, he tested how loose he had me. Stars were shooting in front of my eyes as those large thumbs moved in sync to work me open even more before he finally settled me back over his cock. I braced my hands-on Christian's shoulders as he slowly lowered me onto his rod while pushing his hips up to meet my hole.

With a soft moan, I bit my lip and accepted the burning

stretch as I took him all the way inside of me. It didn't take long for me to adjust to his girth once I sat still for a moment and allowed myself to bask in the feeling of being filled by my alpha.

Running my hands down from his shoulders to his chest, I gripped his pecs and flicked my thumbnails across those taut nipples while I slowly raised up on my knees. Holding eye contact I lowered and raised myself slowly while he guided me with his hands firmly gripped on my hips.

I gritted my teeth against the urge to cry out as his fat cock head grazed my prostate. My senses lit up with each brush of his cock against that little magic bundle of nerves. I began speeding up, chasing the lightening that was just out of reach. My eyes fell closed and my breathing sped up as I increased the rhythm. Fuck. Yes. My core tightened as fire ran down my spine, directly to my dick.

Gasping with pleasure, my hips undulated in a rolling motion as I rode the cock that my alpha was thrusting into me with each movement of our hips. "Open your eyes," he commanded quietly.

My eyes popped open to see him watching me with hooded eyes. His lips twitched into a grin as he panted: "Rub your belly for me. Let me watch you rub it while I fuck your tight ass, babe."

I ran my hands in slow circles, wide to small and all

around in different poses as I showcased the baby bump that was turning him on so much. "Fuck yeah, Liam. You're such a fucking sexy omega!"

He gripped my hips a little harder and began lifting me up and down faster, literally fucking himself with my hole. The way he suddenly took command of my body like I was his personal fucktoy just pushed me over the edge. My vision blurred and all sound turned to white noise as I opened my mouth in a silent scream and shot my load all over the front of my alpha.

I was halfway through covering him with my cream, when I felt a burst of hot cum filling my ass. His face was contorted with pleasure, sweat covering his body as he rutted faster into me while he emptied himself inside my channel.

When we both finished, I flopped forward and collapsed into the mess I'd made all over the front him. He chuckled and rubbed his hands up my back tenderly. I wanted to kiss him, but I was just an over-cooked noodle at this point.

I kissed the side of his throat instead, murmuring: "I love you, Christian. That was definitely worth the wait."

He craned his neck to kiss the top of my head. "Yeah, it was. But round 2 is gonna have to be in the shower. We're both a couple of sticky ass messes."

I snorted. "Yeah, but first we have to dress and get past Kent." He just groaned.

———

January bled into February, and we were sitting in the doctor's office while she squirted cold gel across my belly. I was six months along now, and we were finally going to find out the gender. We could have done it sooner, but this was the first time that we'd been able to coordinate our schedules to both be there at the same time.

Dr. Greene, my new OB/GYN was doing the ultrasound herself in the office today. She ran the wand over my much larger bump and soon the familiar whooshing noise and rapid heartbeat filled the room. I smiled and squeezed Christian's hand as we watched the image appear on the monitor.

The doctor stopped and made a few measurements, entering them into the computer before she moved on. "Here we go, gentlemen. Let's see if the baby wants to cooperate and show us what we're looking for today, shall we?"

I was holding my breath as she showed us a few different things, then she stopped and smiled. "Aha, there she is! Congratulations, daddies. You have a little girl."

Christian and I looked at each other with delight. "Can

you believe it?" He asked happily. "We're having a girl!"

"Yeah, it's what Otis said months ago. He told me my belly had girl written all over it!"

Dr. Greene snorted as she printed off a couple pictures for us and proceeded to put things away and wipe my belly clean. "That reminds me of this one old codger that used hang around the hospital lobby. His name was Otis too. He was a delightful man with a heart of gold. We just had a hard time keeping the old rascal in his room. He had this old leather jacket that he adored. Otis would wear it right over his hospital gown when-ever he was admitted. And if he wasn't sneaking outside for one of his legendary cigars, he was visiting the other patients. He correctly predicted the baby's gender of every pregnant person he came across. It was an eerie gift, trust me."

A shiver ran up my spine and I asked. "Really? What happened to him? Does he still live around here?"

She smiled sadly. "Only if you count Hollydale Ceme-tery as a place of residence. He died about ten years ago of cancer, the poor dear. But he was still smiling and positive until the day he left us, let me tell you. Oh, he'd bluster, fuss, and grumble, but that was just his way."

After that, she gave us our pictures and gave me instructions to follow until my next visit. Once she'd left the room and I was getting dressed again, I looked over at Christian. "That whole Otis thing is just a super weird coincidence, right?"

He nodded with a weird look on his face. "I really want to agree, so very badly. But wasn't it you who were telling me not that long ago that there's no such thing as coincidence?"

I had no reply to that one.

CHAPTER 13

CHRISTIAN

The whole Otis maybe being a dead Otis thing rocked me deeper than I wanted to let on. For one thing, I didn't want to upset my pregnant mate, and for another, I just really didn't want to think about it too closely.

I'd already clued into the whole feathers and Otis connection. I mean, the man had been around every time right before I'd found one. And he'd had that odd habit of popping up and then disappearing again just as quickly.

Although, I had to admit that the idea of that crusty, adorable little man being an angel was just hysterically funny. But even if this was a case of mistaken identity and coincidence, there was no denying that he'd been a guardian angel of sorts to my mate.

On our way home, Liam spoke up and asked: "Have

you given any thought to when you want to get married?"

I shrugged. Now that he wore my ring, I figured the wedding was just a formality. "Not really. Why? Do you?"

Liam nodded. "Yeah, I want to do it soon. I think it's a big deal to Kent that we are married before our little girl gets here. You and I may not be too worried about the legality of it all, but it matters to Kent."

I nodded, touched that my mate was concerned about my brother's feelings. "Okay. And do you know where you might want to do it?"

"Actually? I do. I was talking to Tom, and he's all over helping me make it happen if you agree. Tom said that the city would need to sign off on it, but we can apply for a permit at the same time that we go for our marriage license."

I had a feeling where he was going with this now but had to ask. "And where is it that you want to get married, babe? And more importantly, when?"

"I want to have a small ceremony in the alley where we met. Everything important after I got here happened in that little square area. And, I'd like to do it as soon as we can pull it together. What do you say?"

I pulled over into the turning lane and waited for the light to change so that I could do a U-turn. "I say let's go over to city hall right now, so that we can apply for a license and a permit."

The look on Liam's face said it all, but he spoke anyway. "I knew that I could count on you, alpha."

As it turned out, both the permit and wedding license were easily attained. We ended up picking a week from Saturday when they made us choose a permit date. We'd picked that day after I'd made a quick call to Reverend Ray and that was the only date in the next two months that he was free to marry us.

Since I didn't know any other ministers, I'd chosen to go with him. Besides, I really liked the guy and the things he did for the needy. I felt like he was the perfect person to marry us.

I called Kent before we left the courthouse and gave him the news, so that he could plan to have that Saturday off work. Tom heard Kent's half of the conversation and insisted on talking to Liam right then and there. Apparently, they would have a lot to do in a short amount of time according to Tom. Kent and I didn't bother arguing.

When Tom came on the line, I passed the phone to Liam and started the drive home. By the time we got back to our apartment, they pretty much had everything decided on and made plans to go shopping over the weekend.

I grinned as I parked and saw the page of notes that Liam had made on the notepad app on his phone while he'd busily chatted on mine. One of these days, I might just have to train Liam to work in my office if he was that good at multitasking.

I smiled and leaned back in my seat, picturing Liam working in my office. I'd be free to actually work on cars like I did when I first opened the garage, while my omega was right there running the office and dealing with the dreaded paperwork. I bet he'd even be able to soothe the people who were pissed when their cars were running late due to back-ordered parts and other random bullshit.

Ooh. And when it was slow we could go in the office and lock the door. I reached down to adjust myself as I pictured bending Liam over my desk and pounding into him while the noise of the garage drowned out his screams.

I turned to share my idea with Liam, only to see him watching me with amusement. He was holding out my phone with a quirked brow. "I don't know where you went just then, Christian. But since I'm pretty sure it involved me? Why don't we go upstairs and lay down? We can celebrate having a license to marry while you tell me all about what got you going over there while I was on the phone."

Opening my door, I took my phone from his outstretched hand and hopped out of the car. Right before I closed my door, I leaned into the car where Liam was still staring at me in amusement. "Last one naked in bed gets to come first." I winked and closed the door, deliberately taking small steps. I grinned when I heard the door of my rarely used car slam shut as Liam came barreling toward me.

I laughed and lifted him up in my arms as he tried to get past me. As I swung him up and spun him around, he began smacking my shoulder as he squealed in my ear. "Do you know how pregnant I am? First you challenge me to a race, then you try to give me a heart attack?"

The best way to stop his terror-ranting was to kiss him. After I pressed my lips to his, he squirmed a little more but the smacking slowed before coming to a stop as he began kissing me back. Breaking the kiss, I pulled back with a grin.

"Sorry I scared you, babe. I figured out that if we ended up there at the same time, we could just come together." Liam grinned in response and silently pointed to the stairs. Oh, yeah. I loved having a pregnant omega. Not only was he sexy as fuck, he was always horny.

———

I don't know how they pulled it off, but the alley was

gorgeous for our wedding. Kent and I walked out together from my shop, as we'd been instructed and we both took a gasp as the beauty of it all hit us both all over again. The alley was covered in AstroTurf, with a long red carpet leading from my back door to the altar that had been set up in front of where I knew the dumpsters were located.

The dumpsters were blocked off by a series of eight-foot-tall, mint colored cardboard panels. There was a trellis with silk red roses woven through different places of the cross woven wooden strips. There was no discernible pattern to it, which made it look natural and charming. A gauzy mint chiffon ribbon was threaded through among the roses, combining the two colors we'd chosen for our wedding.

The altar itself was just a wooden platform, draped in the same red carpeting. Reverend Ray was already standing there under the trellis, patiently waiting for the two grooms and their best men.

I looked around while I waited for Liam to appear, taking in all the little details he'd put into our small wedding. The red carpet led off from the altar in the other direction that went to the back door of Sweet Ballz. Our guests were all seated on white folding chairs on the other side of the red carpet, directly opposite the altar.

We hadn't invited a lot of people, since Liam didn't know anyone really outside of our small circle. My employees and their significant others or dates were all there. Milo and Rafe were there with their son. Cecil was there, along with a few people who did know Liam through the store. A few of the local merchants that were friends of mine had decided to come, as well as a few of my customers. When word had traveled about our unique mating and sudden wedding, our phones had gone nuts with people practically inviting themselves.

There were tables set up behind the chairs with finger sandwiches, different platters of finger foods and dips, and of course, trays of various sweet ballz. In the center was a three-tiered white wedding cake with mint green trim and red roses cascading down the front. Two little grooms decorated the top.

A few small stacks of mint green paper plates and red napkins with silver embossing with our names and the date stood there next to a large silver cake knife. There was another table with a large punch bowl sitting next to a large coffee urn, and all the required cups, stirrers, and packets of add-ins.

Yet another table stood off to the side with a mound of gifts stacked on it, and a basket of favors at the other end that we would send home later with each guest. The favors were mint green organza bags filled with miniature Cider Ballz to represent our two scents.

A red ribbon was used to tie little tags to each bag with our names and wedding date on one side and on the other was printed: *"Apple and Cinnamon, the perfect marriage of scents and flavors"*. Apparently, my brother had held back a bottle of the cider to surprise me with these ballz for my birthday but it had gone to use for our wedding favors instead.

I looked around, amazed by how perfect everything was for our wedding. Liam and Tom had worked hard to make this happen. I'd wanted to help, but Liam had shooed me off to work while the omegas took control. Kent said it had been nice to have his boss Milo around the shop again while Tom had been preoccupied with our wedding. I was just glad that my heavily pregnant mate had a good friend to help him pull off his vision for our special day.

I was aware of a flash going off as the hired photographer took pictures while I watched Liam finally walk out onto his end of the red carpet with Tom at his side. He looked gorgeous in a black tux, with a mint green vest and a red rose in his lapel that was identical to my own. We had opted for the vests, or so I was told, because it was more photo friendly to my pregnant omega.

His gorgeous hair was down today, its natural waves combed and forced into submission so that it hung straight and neat across his shoulders. Our eyes met as he walked confidently toward the altar, a look of love passing between us that had my heart racing. Liam and

Tom took their places beside me and Kent, and the ceremony began. It was brief, but poignant.

As I took Liam's hands to make our vows, a plume of smoke caught my eye. I glanced over and saw Otis standing behind the other guests, leaning between the food and gift tables. He grinned back at me with a flash of yellow teeth. Liam saw me looking and sent a wide smile to Otis who looked just as thrilled when he smiled back.

Pulling my attention back to the ceremony, I said my vows to Liam.

"Liam, my love. I vow to love you and protect you as my omega, my husband, and my mate. I vow to be a good father to every child born of your womb, and to treasure each child that we may have as jewels from heaven. You and our children will never fail to have my love, protection, and undying devotion for as long as I shall live."

Liam said his vows next. He had tears in his eyes after hearing mine. I squeezed his trembling hands to encourage him as he took a steadying breath. He looked up at me then with such pure trust in his eyes. To have earned his trust after all he'd been through just touched my heart in ways that I could never explain.

"Christian, I stand here today in front of these witnesses with our daughter inside me and vow that I will love you and cherish you as my alpha, my husband, and my mate. I vow to be a good life partner. To lighten your load wherever I can and to be your help-meet during the hard times that life will bring along the way. I will be by your side with my respect, love, and devotion as long as I shall live."

After our vows were exchanged, Kent and Tom passed us our rings. Once our rings were on our fingers, Reverend Ray said: "Christian and Liam, I now pronounce you husbands and mates. Alpha, you may now kiss your omega."

That may have been what he said, but apparently it wasn't what my husband heard. As soon as Reverend Ray said kiss, Liam flung himself at me, practically climbing me like a tree as he went for the kiss that would seal our ceremony. I grinned against his lips, then dipped him back over my arm and kissed him the way that he needed to be kissed.

Once I stood him up and helped him balance, a laughing Reverend Ray said the best words I'd ever heard strung together. "Ladies and gentlemen, allow me to introduce you to Mr. and Mr. Christian and Liam Hawkins."

When Liam had told me that he'd be taking my name, I hadn't been surprised given his parents treatment of him. Yet, I'd been humbled. He wasn't only taking my name, he was giving his unborn child my name, and showing me that he accepted me as our daughter's other father. So yeah, I'd never been more humbled in my life.

We both made a beeline toward Otis, but got waylaid by the crowd. By the time we made our way back there, he was gone. I grinned at Liam and pointed to the ground. There was a fucking feather lying there where he'd been standing. I bent and picked it up, then tucked it into Liam's lapel behind the rose. When my husband smiled fondly at it, I knew I'd done the right thing.

We made it through the reception, accepting hugs and congratulations from our guests. Almost as soon as the cake was cut and we'd fed each other bites, Tom swept in to save the day. He whispered to us that he would save us cake and all the leftover favors would be at our apartment along with the gifts when we returned from our honeymoon.

He turned then and let out a piercing whistle to get everyone's attention. "Thanks for coming to see the studly Christian marry the fabulous Liam. Now, nobody stop the grooms to talk! Christian and Liam are leaving to go fuck now! The grooms are fulfilling the legal requirement that the marriage be consummated, so none of that snickering! Tom sees that giggling, Grandma! Now, everyone just wave while the grooms make a getaway, m'kay? Bye-bye boys, enjoy the week long schlongfest...or honeymoon, as Tom supposes it's called if one must be boring."

Liam flushed bright red while I choked back a laugh. I

took advantage of the crowd laughing at Tom's speech and swept him up in my arms. I headed down the alley toward where I'd parked my car. The speech worked, because everyone just waved instead of trying to stop us. I had to remember to send Tom a gift card or something when we got back.

CHAPTER 14

LIAM

The two months after our wedding and honeymoon to Cancun flew by while Christian and Kent got us moved into our new house. It was actually in the suburban neighborhood on the other side of the sound wall that ran along the alley. Just another way that the alley tied in with my life here in Hollydale.

Our new house was a four bedroom that faced the sound wall, putting it within walking distance of work for both alphas. I was no longer working, business had slowed for now anyway so Cecil was fine. I was just too tired, too fat, too swollen, too pregnant. Not to mention the fact that I seriously couldn't remember shit anymore. Seriously. I'd fight to get up to go do something, only to forget what I needed by the time I was up. But I'd just go pee then, since I was up anyway and I had to pee every thirty seconds now.

My favorite part of the new house was the private en suite bathroom in the master bedroom. No more sharing a bathroom with my brother-in-law or trying to sneak in to clean up after sex without him seeing us. Kent and Tom had gone overboard setting up our baby girl's nursery. They'd begged, and I couldn't find a good reason to refuse them.

"Hey, babe. Why the deep thought? You need anything?" I looked up from my cup of cocoa to see my alpha standing there looking tasty, covered in sweat and grease from his day at work.

"I was just thinking about how much I love our new house and how fast the past two months have flown by." I smiled and reached for the waistband of his jeans, pulling him closer to me.

Christian grinned down at me. "Yeah, they have. Ollie will be here before we know it."

I glared up at him. "I swear on all that's holy, alpha. I am not naming our daughter Olivia if you're going to insist on calling her Ollie!"

He laughed. "Okay, okay. I won't call her that...when you're around."

Narrowing my eyes, I reached up and grabbed his crotch with a tight grip. "Say that again, my love. Would you like to see what happens when you test the patience of a pregnant omega who's high on hormones and low on give-a-damn's?"

Gently removing my hand, my alpha leaned over and kissed me. "I bet I can find a better use for my cock than it being squeezed by your fist. Wait. That still didn't sound bad. Hmm. I guess it sounds better in theory than in practice?" He stopped and shook his head, as if clearing away the cobwebs.

"That was my unsexy way of inviting you to come take a nap with me."

"But I already had a nap while you were at work. And dinner is in the crockpot. It will be ready in an hour."

"I didn't mean a sleeping nap."

I stared at him, then noticed the bulge in his pants had grown. "OH! Yes, let's take a nap. But first, help me up or you'll be done before I ever get in there."

Christian grinned and just lifted me up in his arms like he loved to do. He carried me into our bedroom and hesitated between the bed and bathroom. "Shower or bed? I'm pretty sweaty and these clothes are filthy. They're pretty much covered in grease and gunk from work."

"Are you being serious right now? You know how much I love you all sweaty and dirty. Now come on, Daddy needs some action."

My alpha grinned and began to strip off his dirty clothes, before reaching over and helping me out of mine. He left me laying on the edge of the bed and stepped in between my legs. After bending over my huge mound of baby to give me a long kiss, he pulled back and grabbed the lube from the nightstand then knelt between my legs.

Christian was tall enough that his crotch was level with the edge of our bed when he knelt beside it. Scooting close, he rubbed a little lube in his hands before taking us both in his strong grip.

"Oh, fuck," I moaned. "That's nice, babe."

I laid there, gripping the blanket in my fists while he stroked us together firmly. Every upstroke, our cocks pushed together to break through the opening in his fist. It was the best fucking sensation. Too soon, I felt my balls tightening. Right as I was mid-moan and about to let it fly, he stopped short.

I panted. "No, I was right there!"

"And you'll get there. Just not yet. I want you to not just see stars. I want you to see the fucking moon, babe."

Oh, shit. I gasped as his lubed finger entered my tight pucker. He worked my hole expertly, before adding a second finger and scissoring them to help open me up for him. When the third finger came into play, I was writhing against the mattress. Every third thrust in with his fingers, he turned his wrist and rubbed against my prostate.

Right as I was about to shoot from the magic button massage, he stopped short again and pulled his hands out. I heard the click of the lube cap again, as he began to slick his cock. Finally! I wanted to reach for my cock to stroke it but couldn't reach it under my big ass belly.

Before I could whine or beg, he was sliding that fantastic cock into me. My alpha reached under my thighs and ran his hands slowly up the length of my legs until he had my ankles in his grip. Holding my legs up and out in a wide vee, he fucked me hard and fast. In this position, I couldn't do anything other than fist the blankets and enjoy the ride.

I turned my head toward the mirrored closet doors, watching his ass muscles flex with each fast pump of his hips. I moved my hands to my tender nipples, playing with them while I floated in a white space of pure pleasure.

Slam, slam, slam, his hips just slammed against me with each thrust. Slap, slap, slap, his balls slapped up against my ass cheeks with each pounding entry. Christian saw where I was looking and turned his head to watch us fucking in the mirror. We caught each other's gaze as I felt his cock swell harder within me.

My cock was bouncing around all over the place from the force of his rutting. My cock started shooting like a sprinkler, flinging spurts of thick cream all over my belly, his chest, his face, even my left knee got a bit. With a loud roar, Christian's head rolled back. He pushed his cock deep inside me, hips twitching as he filled me with his seed.

As he came back to himself, Christian lowered my legs and gently pulled out of my ass. He bent to kiss the inside of each knee before he stood. Tenderly, he lifted my limp body and carried me to the shower.

After he had me nice and clean, Christian turned and quickly washed his own body before turning off the water. He stepped out and grabbed us towels, handing me one to use while he wrapped his own around his waist.

Once I was ready, my alpha lifted me out of the shower and carried me to the bed. He stopped halfway there and looked at me curiously. "Babe, I thought you dried off all the way. You're dripping all over me and the rug, let's go back and grab your towel. I'll help you."

I bent over against his shoulder as an agonizing pain hit me. "Christian, I don't think it's shower water that's dripping."

"Liam. Water is water. Call it whatever, but it's from your shower."

I shook my head. "No, it's not. Listen to me. It's MY water, the baby is coming."

Christian went pale and stepped over to set me down on the bed. He swiped a hand over his hip where some of the water had splashed. Sniffing it, he looked at me and said: "Liam. That's not shower water."

"Duh, babe. Now that we're on the same page, will you help me dress so we can go to the hospital?"

Christian blushed and flew into gear. He got us both dressed in short order and was carrying me out to the car when Kent came walking up the drive. Christian stopped him. "Kent! The baby is coming! Get the passenger door open for me so I can get Liam to the hospital!"

Kent sprang into action. While Christian was a floundering mess, Kent shocked me by taking things in hand and calmly directing his brother. Kent took my mate's keys, stating flatly: "You're in no condition to drive. Do you have your wallet with the insurance cards and your phone?"

Christian was frantically patting his pockets while Kent merely rolled his eyes and took off at a jog to the house. He was back seconds later. After ordering his older brother into the backseat, Kent got in behind the wheel and grinned at me as he passed me Christian's wallet and phone. "You should probably hold onto these for now, the dumb fuck didn't even shut the front door. You're lucky that I got home on time, Liam."

I didn't argue because the young alpha had a point. He got me to the hospital in record time, pulling up in front of the emergency department. Christian jumped right out and ripped my door open. Lifting me up into his arms, he kicked the door shut behind him, silencing the sound of his brother's laughter.

Once we got inside, thankfully, the nurses took over. I had been having a nonstop cycle of painful contractions the whole way over. As soon as I described that to them, they took me straight to an exam room where my husband helped me into a gown.

By the time Kent had the car parked and was inside, I was already pushing. They had patiently explained that first babies come late, and I was still two weeks early so I probably wasn't as far along as I thought.

The ER doctor examined me anyway, while the nurses called the paternity area to let them know I'd be coming up. Except I didn't. I was already crowning when the doctor raised my hospital gown to check to see if the opening to my uterus had become accessible for delivery.

In male omegas, the uterine tube only opened during our heat or for delivery. It was accessible through the same chamber used by the colon, but it was located much lower. When it opened, a flap of tissue blocked the colon so that the chamber was only in use by the uterine tube.

I remembered hearing about it in eighth grade biology, but they hadn't told us how much it would FUCKING HURT! The doctor only had time to get one glove completely on and the other halfway on when the baby's head pushed right through my completely opened ring of muscle.

Nobody had told me to push, but I was consumed by this biological urge to push that I couldn't have kept my body from obeying if I'd tried. One minute I was breathing through a contraction, and the next I was bearing down hard with all of my lower muscles. I looked up at the ceiling and screamed at the top of my lungs: "FUCKING ALPHAS!"

Christian looked startled and the doctor looked horrified as he hurriedly reached to catch the baby that was pushing right out of my body in one smooth push. I leaned back against the gurney that was thankfully propped up behind my back. Gasping for breath, I looked at Christian's face and followed it to see the miraculous creature the doctor was holding.

The rest of the delivery was a blur after Olivia Jane was laid on my chest. Even though she was all goopy and covered with a coating of white funk, blood, and gore; she was still the most beautiful thing that I'd ever laid eyes on. I reluctantly let her go with the nurses to get cleaned up. Christian knelt beside my gurney with tears running down his face.

"Liam," he breathed. "That was the singularly most miraculous thing that I have ever seen in my life. I'm sorry I lost my shit earlier. But I promise, I'm going be the best dad to Olivia Jane. That's my princess right there."

"Oh, fuck, alpha! Why did you have to go and be every kind of awesome while all these hormones are flooding my body?" I laughed as I unsuccessfully pushed away the flood of tears that kept pouring from my eyes.

"I mean it, Liam. That baby may not have come from my loins, but she's the child of my heart. She needs a dad, and I need to be her dad. I've loved her since I first felt that tiny bump hit against me that day we met. I just want you to know how humbled I am that you chose me to be your alpha. You gave me not only the tremendous gift of a mate, but you've chosen to share your precious child with me too. I promise to live my life making sure that you never regret this for even a nanosecond."

"Oh, alpha! Shut up and kiss me!" I reached for him, and he stood to lean over me. Holding me tightly in his arms, I felt the security, love, and devotion that he offered not only to me, but to our child as well.

"And Christian?"

"Yeah, babe?"

"If I'm ever pregnant again, I want Kent around when I get close to delivering. That guy is a fucking rockstar in an emergency!"

Christian snorted out a laugh. We pulled apart as the

nurse came up with Ollie. Olivia! Dammit. That silly nickname wasn't going to be a thing!

Olivia was all wrapped up like a burrito in a hospital blanket. They asked if I was planning to try to breast-feed, a process that while technically possible for omegas was iffy at best. Unfortunately, we just couldn't make enough milk to keep the baby hydrated, let alone keep them fed.

Some omegas pumped their milk and mixed it with a high protein formula to make a blend. After months of research, I'd decided to allow myself the freedom to say no to societal pressure. I had chosen the brand of formula that had the best reviews from doctors and omegas alike. Besides. I liked the idea that Christian would be able to feed her just as freely as I could.

I told the nurse firmly that I would not be nursing and allowed them to make a bottle for our princess. While they were getting the bottle, a nurse from the registration desk poked her head in. I looked up from Olivia to see what the hell this bitch wanted that she would interrupt our private family moment.

When she held out a hospital bracelet and explained apologetically that I'd been so close to delivery that the registration hadn't been completed, I felt badly. Smiling a little kindlier now, I held a wrist out for her to snap my bracelet on. She had a matching little anklet that she put on Olivia. Apparently, my daughter and I would be spending the night here at the hospital.

Christian finally got to hold her while I went over all the paperwork and filled out the forms for her birth certificate. I was jealous that I wasn't the one holding her, until I looked over at them. She was snuggled against his chest, sound asleep. Her lips were a little rosebud that trembled sweetly with each breath.

The nurse finally left, with Kent coming in past her. He looked shy, but I waved him over. "Get in here, Uncle Kent! This is family time, and you're family."

He smiled, his arms full of a bouquet of roses and a teddy bear as big as Olivia that was wearing a little leather jacket. Christian looked over at the things in Kent's arms. "Dude, when did you find time to go gift shopping? You shouldn't have."

Kent shrugged, "I didn't. I was sitting out in the lobby. There was this cool old guy there. We were talking while you were back here having Ollie."

"Olivia," I interrupted, then motioned for him to continue.

Both alphas grinned. "Anyway, after you screamed 'fucking alphas' so loud that everyone stopped and stared over this way and started laughing, he grinned and stood to go. He had this stuff with him. He said they were for you. I was to tell the kiddo that he told him that belly screamed girl and to never doubt a master. And I'm supposed to tell sonny boy that he's proud of him for stepping up."

We were both staring at Kent now. I gulped and looked at the bear a little closer. It was identical to the jacket that Otis wore, just not as worn and cracked with age. Kent set everything down on the foot of my gurney and said: "But hey, enough about your friend. By the way, Tom and Cecil are coming by in a few hours after you're settled into a room. I promised I'd text them when we have a room number."

Kent stopped then, pulling a familiar looking feather out of the inner pocket of his jacket. "Check out this awesome feather I found on the floor by that old guy's chair a few minutes after he left! He must have dropped it, I dunno. But have you ever seen anything this special? I mean, just look at it!"

Christian had already shown me his collection of feathers. I even had the one we'd found at the wedding pressed under the glass with our large wedding portrait. He and I just looked at the feather, then back at each other, and we both started laughing while Kent stood there looking confused.

"It's okay, Kent. We're not laughing at your feather." Christian said after he calmed down because Ollie...shit! Olivia! started to stir. "Remind me to tell you a story sometime about those feathers. But enough about that for now. Come on over and sit down on this extra chair here. Let me introduce you to your niece."

CHAPTER 15

CHRISTIAN

"There you go, princess! That's it! Lift that foot, come to Daddy." I knelt across from my husband as our little girl went back and forth between us, showing off her new trick of mobility. Her little arms flailed around in the air as she balanced on her tiptoes, listing wildly from side to side as she tried to find her equilibrium.

It was adorable. She was half walking, half running as she dashed across the room joyfully testing her legs. I looked over at Liam with a big grin. I caught her as she started to pitch forward, lifting her high above my head before setting her down facing her Papa. She did the return trip a little more steadily this time.

"You know, if she keeps this up she's gonna be walking at her birthday party next week, Liam."

My mate nodded happily. "I'm pretty sure she will be,

you know? Just this morning she was still feeling her way along the furniture."

"Well, all I know is, her daddies need to let me know what kind of cake I'm baking for my niece." Kent came in right then and set down his keys. He went over and crouched beside Liam. His arms came out and our baby girl ran right into them.

Liam snorted. "Ollie, you're such a traitor. Always with your Uncle Kent. What am I, chopped liver?"

As soon as he said the words chopped liver, I could tell he regretted it. He jumped up and left Kent holding Ollie, as she was now universally known. Liam clamped a hand over his mouth and dashed down the hall to the bathroom.

Kent winced in Liam's direction as he stood up with Ollie on his hip. "Poor Liam. How much longer did the doctor say this should last? I don't remember him puking all the time the last time he was pregnant."

I shook my head. "From what Liam has said, we met him right after that part ended. But yeah, I guess it lasted the whole first trimester with Ollie."

Kent shuddered. "Damn. And everyone says that we alphas are the tough ones. Can you even imagine going through all that? I mean, even if it does give you a cute little thing like our Princess Ollie. I don't care who thinks I'm weak, I know I could never deal with that shit."

Ollie squealed "Sheee". Kent and I exchanged a horrified look, Oh, fuck. If our daughter's first actual word was a variation of the word *shit*? Liam actually would kill us. Dead. And given the fact that he was pregnant again with our second child? It would depend on his hormonal fluctuations whether or not he made us suffer first.

I looked at Kent and said softly: "This never happened, it was a random sound. And from now on, no cussing around Ollie. Deal?"

Kent nodded with relief. He was as afraid of my sweet little omega's temper as I was. It wasn't that Liam was mean. It was that look of disappointment he shot you. Man, that shit was effective! Both of us tried never to disappoint our Liam. He was precious to both of us.

Liam came back down the hall, his hand on his hip with a smirk on his face. He held up his baby monitor, the twin to the one that was sitting on the coffee table just out of Ollie's reach. Except that his was in receive mode, and ours was in send mode. We did this when we were downstairs so that we could hear if one of us needed help with Ollie.

I blushed and tried to look innocent. Liam surprised us both by giggling. "I agree with the no more cussing rule, Uncle Kent. But I have a confession to make. I said it myself a couple of days ago. She's been making the sound off and on ever since. The only thing you did was reinforce a word she'd already heard."

Kent snickered and walked over to kiss Liam on the forehead. "Thanks for telling us that, Liam. Seriously. Now, I not only don't need to feel guilty, but I have something to remind you about the next time I goof up."

Liam stuck his tongue out at Kent. "Just for that, you get to deal with nap time. I need to lay down and I really need to steal your brother to come cuddle with me."

Kent smiled gently at my mate. "Liam. Go rest. Take my alphahole brother with you. I've got Ollie. We'll be fine. I promise. There will be no booze-soaked parties or tiny drool covered fingers in electric sockets. You can trust me. You know that."

With a soft smile, Liam stood on tiptoes and kissed Kent's cheek. "I do know that, Kent. And thank you. When I'm feeling better, I'm going to owe you the dinner of your choice. Deal?"

Kent nodded. "Deal. And since we all know it's your fried chicken, we'll just plan on that one, right?"

Liam laughed and reached out for my hand. I stood and walked over to him. I leaned in and gave my princess a kiss on her chubby little cheek. Fingering one of her soft brown ringlet curls, I smiled at her before thanking Kent.

With my arm around my mate, we walked back to our room the way we walked through life. Arm in arm. Side by side. Liam was my omega. My mate. My husband. The father of my children. And pretty much the best damn thing that had ever happened to me.

I had no doubt that Otis was an angel, even if we never of it spoke it out loud. Because it only made sense to me that it would take an angel to deliver this angel into my life. I had no idea what I'd ever done to deserve him, but I was willing to spend the rest of my life making sure that our angel never doubted that he'd chosen the right alpha.

Fin

AUTHOR'S NOTE

Thank you for reading *Cinnamon Spiced Omega.* If you've enjoyed this book, please leave a review recommending this story to other readers. Make sure to mention your favorite part; I always look forward to reading reviews! If you'd like to know who gets a happy ending next in The Hollydale Omegas, keep reading for a sneak preview of *Peppermint Spiced Omega.*

CHAPTER 16

COLIN

I walked into the crowded O-zone Lair, or Big O as we locals call it, and looked around the packed club. I made a beeline for my favorite seat at the end of the long mahogany bar. My buddy Greg was manning the bar tonight. Before my butt was all the way on the cracked vinyl cushion of the worn out stool, he had a full draft poured and was sliding it across the counter.

It had been a long sucky-ass grind of a week and all I wanted was a cold beer, a hot omega, and three days of uninterrupted sleep. I couldn't do much about the latter two items, but I sure as hell could get a drink.

"How's it hanging, doc? Just ending another week of strutting around that big fancy hospital like you're God's gift to the nurses?" He took the $50 bill I tossed down and put it in the register. Greg would let me know when I needed to kick in more, he was skilled in that department.

I snorted and held up my drink. "Shit. I wish. You don't want to know what my week was like. Let's just say that you read my mind with this and keep 'em coming."

Greg leaned toward me with a leering smirk. "Well, I've got something that might cheer you up. We have a new boy. He's dancing in the cage by the DJ booth tonight. His name's Tofer and he's wearing a bright green jock-strap and enough glitter to make Tinkerbell choke. Or, if blondie isn't what you're looking for tonight, then maybe look out on the dance floor. There's a certain ginger out there that I've seen you eyeballing in the past."

I forced myself not to automatically seek him out. I wasn't going to give Greg the pleasure of knowing he was right. Instead, I gave a noncommittal shrug and took a long drink. After running the back of my hand across my mouth to wipe away the foam, I casually looked around the club.

"He's over there dancing by the caged blonde I mentioned, if you're looking for him." Greg wiped the counter and put a clean dish of nuts in front of me. "By the way, I know you're not interested, but his name is Tom. He manages Sweet Ballz."

I had just taken a drink and pretty much choked when I heard that. Coughing and sputtering, I glared at the smirking little prick. "Seriously? Did you time that shit on purpose? You do know that if you kill me, you won't have a doctor friend the next time you cut your hand on broken glass, right?"

"Aw, come on! That was a one time thing, it could have happened to anyone. There was a broken glass in the dishpan. The fact that I may or may not have been a little bit sloshed at the time and had no business in the kitchen has nothing to do with it."

He studied his hand, looking yet again for the invisible scar that didn't exist because I was just that good. I smirked as I shook my head and popped a handful of nuts into my mouth.

Greg got sidetracked a few minutes later by some other customers, and I took the opportunity to spin on my stool and look around the bar. There he was, just as Greg had said, dancing in front of the big birdcage and laughing with the dancer inside.

The little ginger was glorious. His toned, limber body moved fluidly under the moving lights, not missing a beat while laughing and chatting with the caged blonde. There were seven of the large silver cages spread around this bottom floor area. Each one held an omega dressed in a different color jockstrap with his body painted in glitter to match it. Most of the other cages had alphas swarming around it, except for that one by the DJ booth. There were a few alphas hanging around dancing in the vicinity, but not being creeps about it.

The blonde vaguely reminded me of a dirty elf, for some strange reason. Even from here, I could see that his almond shaped eyes were just a little too big and his nose a little too pointy. Of course, that could just be an optical illusion, brought on by the holly green glitter and jock strap he wore.

A well dressed blonde alpha came walking over and took the stool two down from me. He ordered two straight tequila shooters with beer chasers, then looked over at me with a grin and shoved one set my way.

"Here, man. Don't make me drink alone. It's been a shitty fucking day that topped off a craptastic week." His green eyes sparkled in the light of the bar as we clinked our glasses and did the shot.

I sucked on the little lime wedge that Greg had stuck on the salt coated rim of the glass and held out a hand. "I'm Colin, by the way. Thanks for that, I've had one of those weeks myself."

The other alpha grinned in solidarity and shook my hand. "Ian. Glad to be a bright spot in your week."

"Shit. You have no idea. I was half-assing the idea of picking up an omega for the night, but I think I'm too fried for that shit." I shook my head with a self-deprecating smile and took a pull from my beer.

"I hear you on that one. Rosy Palm is a lot easier when you're worn the fuck out. You don't have to worry about being gentle or if you used enough lube. Rosy don't give a shit about no stinkin' lube." We both laughed at that one.

"So what do you do, Colin? I'm an attorney, myself. I lost a pretty big case in L.A. today. I just got back to town an hour ago. The Big O is always a good place to blow off some steam, right?"

"No, shit. Sorry about your case. I'm a doctor. I work in the emergency room at the hospital here in town. One of my favorite patients, a little girl from the foster system that comes in a lot with different problems, was finally diagnosed today with non-Hodgkin lymphoma. She was admitted to the hospital, and her foster parents are backing away right when she needs someone the most. People fucking suck, you know?"

"You win, dude. Shittiest week award goes to you, doc." Ian frowned sadly at his beer. What I'd shared had been a little heavy for Friday night at the Big O.

Changing the subject, I brought up the latest ballgame. We drank our beers and bullshitted for awhile. We sat with our backs to the bar. I was enjoying the man's company. It was as a good way to unwind as any, I supposed. Ian's eyes flitted around the room, checking out the different omegas but not settling on any one type in particular. I had just ordered another round for me and my new buddy when a familiar red-headed dynamo came flying up out of nowhere.

Practically springing up on tippy-toe, he threw his arms around my neck and planted a big kiss on me. He was wedged in between my open legs. If he got any closer, we'd need some lube so nobody got hurt. I barely had time to register what was happening, let alone respond to the tongue that quickly slipped in and out of my mouth before it was over.

"Sorry to keep you waiting, Daddy. Tom was caught up in the music." He pouted out his words, then turned to do an overly dramatic double take in Ian's direction. "Ian! Tom is so, so sorry! Tom would never flaunt the hot daddy in front of Ian, even if Ian did make stupid choices."

Ian rolled his eyes and gave the ginger twink a lazy grin. "Hey, Tommy boy. Didja miss me? I missed you."

Tom gave Ian a cold eyed smile and waved his fingers dismissively as he spoke in a cheerfully passive aggressive tone. "Has Ian been gone? Tom didn't notice. Hmm. Maybe it could be that Ian was never around enough for Tom to notice one way or the other?"

I was really confused at this point. Was the ginger talking in the third person and his name was Tom? Or was there a third guy they both knew named Tom? Either way, this didn't look amicable and I was a little too buzzed to process subtlety right now.

"Who the fuck is Tom?" I asked a little more rudely than I'd intended.

The ginger looked back at me and turned up the flirt level. His smile was pretty, but didn't reach his eyes. His eyes were blank, like this was just an act for him. I wished I was more sober so that I could try and figure him out better.

"Silly Daddy! Like Daddy doesn't know Tom! Although," he stopped and tapped his lip thoughtfully, "maybe we got to the naughty stuff so fast last time that we never got to the name exchange?"

Ian stood and drained his glass. He looked at me with an insolent grin. "He's all yours, buddy. With my blessings. Consider him your prize for winning the award. I'm done with this on again, off again bullshit. I never wanted more than a fuck buddy anyway. Enjoy him though, he's really bendy if you haven't discovered that yet."

Tom turned his back on the departing alpha without a word and held a hand up to get Greg's attention. I pushed my untouched beer at him.

"Here, kiddo. You look like you can use this more than me. Sorry about that, whatever it was." I hoped that I was speaking clearly. I was getting more buzzed by the second, a fact not helped by my lack of sleep and an empty stomach.

Tom pushed the beer aside and shook his head.

Holding out his hand, he demanded instead, "Give Tom the keys, and let's go. Tom will get the sweet daddy alpha home."

I blinked at him stupidly. "Why would I give my keys to Tom? Could you just take me?"

The ginger giggled wildly and stepped forward. He tugged on my hand to get me up, then dug my keys out of my pocket with nimble fingers. He turned to Greg.

"Did the sexy Daddy here run a tab or does the hot barkeep need Tom's card?"

Greg grinned. "Naw, man. It's cool. Colin gave me enough cash earlier, he's good." He looked over at me with a grin. "You want your change, big guy? This little scene here is all the tip I need."

I flipped him off with a teasing smirk and said, "Here's your tip, fucker. And yeah, keep the fucking change."

Tom pulled on my hand and led me out of the bar. He didn't bother asking which car belonged to me. Instead he clicked the button on my key fob and headed toward the car that reacted.

"Come on, Daddy. Let's roll that tight ass into the car. Is Daddy's GPS set for home, or does Tom need to rely on Daddy's iffy directions?"

I snorted. "I'm buzzed, not shit-faced. I'm pretty sure I can get you to my place. Now what I'm gonna do with you when we get there? Well, that's a whole other question, isn't it?"

Tom flashed me a flirtatious smile that still didn't quite reach his eyes. "If Daddy is awake and can make that alpha equipment work, then Tom will be happy to show Daddy exactly what can be done with Tom."

Stunned into silence, I turned on my GPS and hit home. Tom turned on my radio to some insipid holiday station while I leaned back against the headrest and wondered how the hell I'd managed to score with the hot ginger.

What did you think? Want to know what happens next? You can buy *Peppermint Spiced Omega* right now —just navigate to the link below.

Peppermint Spiced Omega: Book 3
https://amazon.com/dp/B077H1TQW5

Cupid always gives you a second chance…
Join my mailing list and get your FREE copy of
Strawberry Spiced Omega
https://dl.bookfunnel.com/io4ia6hgz8

Twitter:
https://twitter.com/SusiHawkeAuthor

Facebook:
https://www.facebook.com/SusiHawkeAuthor

Alpha's Dream: Book 1

Omega Found: Book 2

Omega's Destiny: Book 3

Alpha's Dom: Book 4

Alpha's Charm: Book 5

Omega's Mark: Book 6

Alpha's Seal: Book 7

The Hollydale Omegas

Pumpkin Spiced Omega: Book 1

Cinnamon Spiced Omega: Book 2

Peppermint Spiced Omega: Book 3

Champagne Spiced Omega: Book 4

Chocolate Spiced Omega: Book 5

Shamrock Spiced Omega: Book 6

Marshmallow Spiced Omega: Book 7

Three Hearts Collection
(with Harper B. Cole)

The Surrogate Omega: Book 1

The Divorced Omega: Book 2

Waking the Dragons

(with Piper Scott)

Alpha Awakened: Book 1

Alpha Ablaze: Book 2

Alpha Deceived: Book 3

Alpha Victorious: Book 4

Team A.L.P.H.A.

(with Crista Crown)

Grabbed: Book 1

Taken: Book 2

MacIntosh Meadows

The Alpha's Widower: Book 1

The Omega's Dance: Book 2

Printed in Great Britain
by Amazon